THE DEATH OF YORIK MORTWELL

Also by Stephen Messer

Windblowne

～ THE DEATH OF YORIK MORTWELL ～

BY STEPHEN MESSER

Illustrated by Gris Grimly

RANDOM HOUSE 🏠 NEW YORK

Text copyright © 2011 by Stephen Messer
Jacket art and interior illustrations copyright © 2011 by Gris Grimly

All rights reserved. Published in the United States by Random House Children's Books,
a division of Random House, Inc., New York.

Random House and the colophon are registered trademarks of Random House, Inc.

Visit us on the Web! www.randomhouse.com/kids

Educators and librarians, for a variety of teaching tools, visit us at www.randomhouse.com/teachers

Library of Congress Cataloging-in-Publication Data
Messer, Stephen, 1972–
The death of Yorik Mortwell / Stephen Messer. — 1st ed.
p. cm.
Summary: Following his death at the hands of fellow twelve-year-old, Lord Thomas,
Yorik returns as a ghost to protect his sister from a similar fate but soon learns of ancient
magical beings, both good and evil, who are vying for power at the Estate.
ISBN 978-0-375-86858-0 (trade) — ISBN 978-0-375-96858-7 (lib. bdg.) —
ISBN 978-0-375-89928-7 (ebook)
[1. Ghosts—Fiction. 2. Good and evil—Fiction. 3. Magic—Fiction. 4. Demonology—Fiction.
5. Brothers and sisters—Fiction. 6. Social classes—Fiction. 7. Fantasy.] I. Title.
PZ7.M554De 2011
[Fic]—dc22
2010014255

Printed in the United States of America
10 9 8 7 6 5 4 3 2 1
First Edition

To Memere

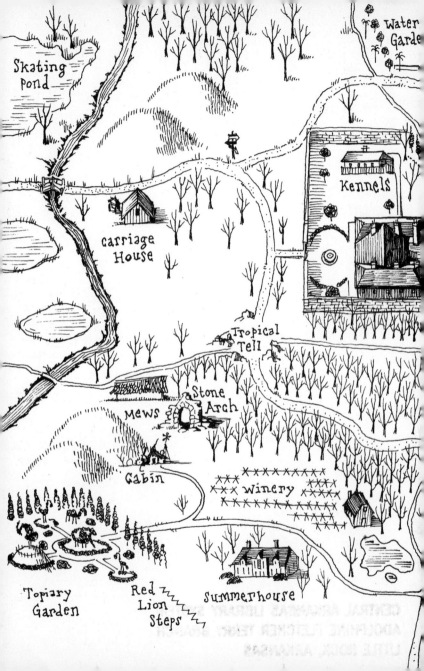

Water Garde

Skating Pond

Kennels

Carriage House

Tropical Tell

Stone Arch

Mews

Cabin

Winery

Topiary Garden

Red Lion Steps

Summerhouse

Servants'
Cemetery

Family
Cemetery

Mooring
Tower

Hedge
Maze

Salt
Springs

Manor

Bottomless
Lake

Wooded
Walk

Shooting
Range

Aviary Glade

THE DEATH OF YORIK MORTWELL

How to Tie a Bowline Knot

The bowline knot, used since the time of
the ancient Egyptians, is known as the king
of knots. Yorik Mortwell tied quite a lot
of them on the last day of his life.

Chapter One

Twelve-year-old Yorik Mortwell lay on the hard, cold ground, dead.

His day had started off rather better than that.

"Come on," he had said to his little sister that morning. "I'll show you how to snare partridges."

They were reluctant to leave the one-room cabin on such a frosty autumn day, when the roaring fire they'd built had warmed that room so nicely, but Yorik knew they needed the food and Susan was always interested in learning about anything and everything. So they bundled up as best they could and went shivering onto the Estate.

They went deliberately along the paths, at first rough and wooded, then finely manicured, then rough and wooded again. They passed the mews and the winery and the fishponds and the shooting range. Through the dense woods they sometimes caught sight of Ravenby Manor, with its twenty-seven chimneys.

Once they heard a muffled droning, and the slim, fleet shape of Lord Ravenby's personal dirigible appeared in the clouds, flying toward its mooring tower in a meadow in the Estate's farthest corner.

"Here," said Yorik, and they plunged off into the trees.

"H-how do you know?" Susan said, teeth chattering. She looked excited, though her lips were blue. Yorik vowed to get her back to the warm cabin as soon as he could.

"I've seen them feeding here," Yorik said. They had come to a small clearing. "Now collect sticks."

Yorik showed Susan how to build a boot-high fence of twigs in a semicircle around the feeding ground. At intervals they left openings for gateways made from sticks bent carefully into arches.

"The partridges will poke their heads through these," explained Yorik.

Susan nodded, concentrating.

Yorik took a long spool of string from one pocket and his knife from the other. He cut several lengths of string, one for each archway. He showed Susan how to tie a bowline knot, reciting:

Lay the bight to make a hole
Then under the back and around the pole
Over the top and through the eye
Cinch it tight and let it lie

Then he slipped the free end of the string back through the loop in order to make a slip noose. They tied that end to the top of the arch. To hold the slip noose open, Yorik cut notches in each side of the arch, then secured the strings in each notch. Susan helped, and soon enough she was tying bowline knots and making slip nooses as though she'd been doing it all her life.

"Once they're in the slip noose," asked Susan, "can't they just back out?"

"They can," replied Yorik, "but they won't. A partridge will keep trying to force its way forward, and the loop will hold it in place until we return."

The work took a long, frigid hour, and by the end their fingers were red and numb and their ears ached from the cold. But they could stand back in pride and admire a perfect partridge snare.

"How lovely," said a nasty voice from behind them. "But those partridges belong to me, you know."

Yorik and Susan turned. A boy stood there, the same age as Yorik, leaning on a walking stick with a ruby knob on one end. Susan curtsied, and Yorik dipped his head. "Yes, Master Thomas," said Yorik.

Master Thomas sauntered forward. He looked considerably warmer than Yorik and Susan. His heavy coat was made of wool, and he wore a fur cap and mittens. A black scarf was wrapped around and around his neck. He was stout to begin with, and these thick layers of clothing gave him the aspect

of a cannonball. Mean eyes
stared out from beneath
the cap.

"What did you in-
tend to do with your
catch?"

"If it please you,
Master," replied Yorik,
"the usual—eight in ten will go to the Estate, and
two to the gamekeeper."

"You're not the gamekeeper." Master Thomas
smiled. "The gamekeeper is dead."

Yorik and Susan stood in a vast, aching silence,
thinking of their father.

Pleased, Master Thomas went on. "You should
consider yourselves fortunate that my father has
allowed you to stay on the Estate at all. And you
repay him by poaching his birds."

"We weren't poaching, sir—" Susan began. But
Yorik put a hand on her shoulder.

They stood shivering and silent as Master
Thomas approached the snare. "Do not gainsay me,
little girl," he said in a tone as cold as the wind that

cut through their clothes. "I say you were poaching. And I won't allow it."

He raised his walking stick and brought it crashing down across the little fence.

Yorik and Susan watched as he walked the length of it, at first bashing with the stick, then simply kicking. By the end, the snare had been scattered and trampled and ground into the earth, an hour's labor gone in less than a minute.

The exertion had cost Master Thomas. He bent over with his hands on his knees, red in the face and breathing heavily, but looking satisfied with his work. When he had recovered, he straightened himself and removed a black handkerchief from within his coat. He blew into it while Yorik and Susan watched helplessly. Then he sighed, tucked the handkerchief away, and looked about as though he had forgotten about Yorik and Susan and was simply enjoying the day.

Finally he began to stride away. "Don't let me catch you at this again," he warned loftily, "or I'll tell my father and he'll have you thrown off the Estate."

Yorik watched the cannonball as it rolled past and receded into the forest.

"You didn't have to do that!" he muttered. Susan stiffened and gave a little whimper.

The cannonball froze, then turned slowly.

Master Thomas walked back to them, swinging the walking stick in a figure eight, the ruby knob leaving a trail as it cut the air. He walked straight up to Yorik and pointed the stick at him.

"Apologize," he commanded.

Seconds passed. Yorik said nothing. He became aware, in that long silence, of distant sounds of the Estate at work, of chopping and barking and the neighing of horses.

Master Thomas pointed the stick at Susan. "Apologize," he said softly.

"I'm sorry," said Yorik.

"Good," said Master Thomas. He looked all around. He looked up. Then he pointed with the stick. "Now fetch me that apple there. I'm hungry."

Yorik and Susan looked up. "What apple?" Yorik said finally.

"The apple in the apple tree," said Master

Thomas patiently. "Fetch it. It's up there at the top."

Yorik waited. Master Thomas watched him. "It's an elm tree," said Yorik.

"It's an apple tree," said Master Thomas. "Now start climbing."

Yorik began climbing the elm, cursing himself for his stupidity in talking back to Family. His father had taught him better.

At last he reached the highest point to which he could safely climb. He looked down to see what his next order would be. Master Thomas had used his time to gather an arsenal of rocks. He began throwing them at Yorik. Yorik tried to get as much of the elm between him and Master Thomas as he could, but there wasn't much tree up there, and Master Thomas was walking around the trunk, taking his time. One rock struck Yorik on the leg, another on the hand.

Susan began to cry.

"Susan, no," said Yorik. "It's all right. It—"

He noticed the rock Master Thomas was holding. Even from high up, he could see it was a big one.

Then Susan had Master Thomas by the arm, struggling and fighting, and Master Thomas gave her a terrific shove that sent her sprawling.

Yorik hurtled down through the branches, everything gone red. He was shouting things, terrible things, and he looked at Master Thomas and saw that the boy had thrown that big rock, and it got bigger and bigger as it came, a large dark blur, and then something happened to the side of his head and he was falling. He was headfirst now, and he could see branches coming up at him. Something happened to his shoulder as it struck one branch, then something to a knee. It hurt awfully. He thought about trying to catch on to one of the branches, but though it seemed that the fall was taking a very long time, it was also happening quickly, and he couldn't quite grab one. He was hitting branches and falling, and then everything simply went black, black as Master Thomas's scarf and handkerchief. His last sight, as life faded out, was that of the big black bulk of Ravenby Manor, and then everything closed onto him.

• • •

Yorik Mortwell lay on the hard, cold ground, dead.

A long time passed.

There were voices.

"What's it?" growled a dark, gravelly one.

"It's a dead boy, silly!" said another one, haughty and refined.

Yorik opened his eyes to see who was speaking.

Chapter Two

Yorik saw crisp winter sky above, and bare elm branches, and he could see where Dark Moon Lilith, forever invisible, blotted out a circle of stars. It was night.

Two startling faces leaned over, blocking his view.

The first face got Yorik's attention immediately. It appeared to belong to a sort of girl—a sort of girl who was about three feet tall, and whose head was squat and round like a common toadstool cap. The rest of her was thin as a stick. Her hair was short, dark, and matted with dirt, and she had bulbous eyes that were entirely brown. They were light brown in the iris, and muddy brown in the pupil.

Then she opened her mouth, and Yorik, had he been alive, would have run away in terror. The girl-creature had three or four rows of teeth all jumbled together, but worst of all, her mouth seemed to be filled with mud.

"'s lookin' at me," the mouth said, and some clumps of mud fell out and onto Yorik. The voice was thick and mumbled, and the dark brown eyes glittered.

"Of course it is!" The other face sniffed. "What wouldn't, with looks like yours?"

Yorik, with great effort, pulled his attention to that one.

This face definitely belonged to a girl—a more normal-looking girl, except that she was extraordinarily pretty, with silver curls. Yorik could see that the hair wasn't silver-colored, but actual silver. He had seen silver once, many years ago, when Mistress Doris, haughty as her younger brother, Thomas, had shown Yorik a silver cup she had stolen from the

Manor's collection. But Doris was long dead of the plague.

The girl with silver curls seemed to be playing dress-up, as she wore a crown in her hair that was made of laurel branches all woven together. Her mouth was pinched into delighted disapproval, as though Yorik were both appalling and necessary.

The faces stared at him. He tried to get up. His arms and legs would not cooperate. He knew they must all be broken. He had clear memories of breaking them one by one as he plunged out of the elm. His shoulder too, and his neck. Nothing worked.

He tried to speak. That, at least, was functional, although his jaw also seemed jammed to one side somehow. "S-Susan," he said thickly.

"Huh!" exclaimed the muddy girl. "Can talk!"

"Of course it can talk, Erde!" Though the pretty girl's tone was rude as ever, it was clear she was getting happier by the second. Her whole face gleamed as she peered at Yorik's broken body. In fact, it did actually gleam, Yorik noticed. It had a shining halo around it—no, not just her face. Her whole body, or as much of it as he could see, shone with silver light. Her dress of gossamer green flashed and sparked.

Yorik tried to turn his head, but his neck was stuck in the wrong position.

"'s no good," grunted Erde, putting her face close to Yorik and sniffing. He wished he could recoil in terror. "'s broken."

"No, it's perfect!" said the haughty girl, delighted. She sounded like the sort of maniacal little noble girl who might visit the Estate, whose laughter would float from the open windows of the Manor but whose face Yorik would never see. "It's a tragically dead boy! Just exactly what we need!"

"Why tragic?" moaned Erde. Erde was a girl's name, but this did not sound like a girl at all. It sounded rumbling and old, like boulders grinding together.

The gleaming girl sighed. "It died before its time! You can tell from looking at it."

"How?"

Light footsteps circled around Yorik. "These usually live seventy or eighty years."

"Not long," grumbled Erde.

"No, it isn't. And this one looks about six."

Twelve! thought Yorik, offended. But he didn't dare contradict this noble-sounding girl.

"What's a susan?" asked Erde.

"Probably a sister," replied the silver girl.

"What's a sister?"

"It means two humans with the same parent," said the girl impatiently. "Stop asking questions."

"We're sisters," rumbled Erde thoughtfully.

"No, we aren't! That's just a stupid human idea. You and I are completely different." The girl's eyes blazed with silver flares. "Especially you."

Yorik worked his mouth again. "Wh-what h-h-happened?" Making words was difficult.

"Do not interrupt me when I'm speaking!" ordered the girl. She raised her arm, which was holding a slender twig with green leaves sprouting off. She waved this at Yorik in a threatening way.

"Tell him!" grunted Erde, waving her arms and hopping.

"Fine," said the silver girl. She lowered the twig and bent close to Yorik. "What happened is that you've died, and it was a really horrible, nasty, tragic death too, by the look of things."

Yorik wondered if he should apologize for that.

The girl looked him over. "You must have fallen from my elm. How many branches did you hit on the way down, anyway? Here, I'll fix that." She brought up the leafy twig and pointed.

Yorik felt the most curious sensation. Warmth spread through his limbs.

"Only my first season here," continued the girl, waving her twig at Yorik, "and already I've found a dead human. You creatures have so little time to live, whatever are you diving out of trees for?"

Something in Yorik's neck popped into place. He realized he could move his arms and legs.

"There!" declared the silver girl with a flourish. "Completely repaired."

"Thank you," Yorik said, sitting up.

"Don't thank me," said the girl. "You work for me now!"

Even in the dark night, Yorik could see everything

perfectly. There were still remnants of the partridge snare scattered around, but they looked weeks old. He guessed, from the dry, snowy scent of the air and the stark, barren elm, that a month or so had passed, and it was now November.

And he was dead.

"I'm a ghost," he said, amazed.

"And I am . . . I am . . ." The girl paused, seeming to think.

Yorik waited.

"The all-powerful Princess of the Aviary Glade!" she announced at last. "That's what you can call me. And you are my servant. Your first order is to haunt the lands of your old human masters."

"You mean the Ravenbys?" asked Yorik.

"Call them whatever you want," the Princess said, swishing her twig. "You're a ghost and you've got to haunt something. But while you're at it, I require you to spy, with your ghosty eyes and ears. I want to know everything you see and hear."

Yorik, who had been a servant his entire life, supposed that it was only natural he would be a servant in death as well. He looked at Erde.

"'m Erde," groaned Erde, hopping. Clumps of dirt fell from her gaping mouth.

"She's not your concern," snapped the Princess. "You will serve me, or . . . or . . ." She looked about. She spied an acorn and snatched it up. "Or I'll imprison you in this acorn forever!"

"You don't have to make threats, Your Highness," said Yorik humbly. "I'll help." He rose gradually to his feet, achingly stretching his creaky limbs.

The Princess looked suspicious. "You'll help me? Just like that?"

"Of course I will. I want to haunt the Ravenbys. I want revenge!"

"You? Whatever do *you* want revenge for?"

"They killed me! Well, one of them did. He knocked me out of the elm with a rock."

"Cor," moaned Erde, dirt dribbling. "'s right."

"Well then," said the Princess, seeming disappointed. She dropped the acorn. "I suppose you've got to haunt him a bit. But I command you to report back to me."

Yorik considered for a moment. "May I ask a question, Your Highness?"

Erde snickered muddily.

The Princess fastened her gaze somewhere above Yorik's head and assumed an imperious air. "There is no need. I already know your question. You wish to know why a being as mighty as I needs a ghost to spy for me!"

"Well, no—" began Yorik.

The Princess stamped her foot. "It's because of beastly Father! He has trapped me in this glade to punish me! I can't do any magic outside of it. If I leave its confines I'll be in terrible trouble. If I hadn't found Erde hiding here, I'd be all alone, not that I would mind. Anyway, this is why your tragic death is perfectly wonderful! I now have a servant ghost-boy who can leave the glade to do my bidding." She waved her twig gleefully, and flowers sprang up all around in full bloom, despite its being November. "There," she said. "I have answered your question."

Actually, she had not. Yorik hesitated. "Your Majesty," he said, "I want to haunt my former human masters, but I don't know how."

The Princess shrugged. "You're the ghost," she said. "Why are you asking me?"

"I've only been a ghost for a few minutes," Yorik replied. "I don't know what to do."

The Princess sighed heavily. "You know. Do ghosty things. Stagger around and moan. Make accusations. Humans are very weak creatures and are easily frightened. You'll hardly have to do anything at all."

Yorik had even more questions now. But he didn't dare ask them. The Princess looked impatient, and Yorik had learned that a servant who questioned his betters would soon regret it.

Instead, he looked at Erde, who was sprawled in the dirt. She was using one of her skinny fingers— almost a claw, really—to draw intricate patterns in the earth. "Are you a servant too?" he asked.

Erde stopped drawing and looked up at Yorik, a fathomless expression on her dirty brown face.

"Of course she's not my servant!" snapped the Princess. "Don't be stupid! That's enough questions. Now, you haunt!"

Chapter Three

Susan.

Though Yorik looked forward to haunting, his first thought was for his sister. As Pale Moon Luna rushed up from the east, he hurried along the deserted paths of the Estate to the cold one-room cabin. But he found the door hanging open, and inside only cobwebs and dust, shuttered windows, and moldy smells. Susan, and everything of the lives they had lived there, had vanished.

With a frozen rage, Yorik swept back through the Wooded Walk, then onto the riding lane, then over the Tropical Tell to the front gates of Ravenby Manor. He stood looking at the tall iron spikes and the ornate *R,* as tall as he. He had never been allowed this close to the Manor, and from here its chimneys, gables, and steeples hulked more ominously than ever. Pale Moon Luna slid behind, transforming the house into black silhouette. High up and far behind the Manor, Lord Ravenby's moored dirigible, the *Indomitable,* drifted like a thundercloud, its landing lights gleaming dimly through low clouds.

Those low clouds floated over the Manor, and where they caught on the points of the steeples, they sent out wispy tendrils like whirlpools across the roofs, lit by moonlight. Sometimes those wisps seemed to form fleeting faces before dissipating into the night. Yorik was transfixed. The Manor was dark, but here and there lamps flickered watchfully from windows.

Yorik reached for the padlocked gates. *I am a ghost.*

As he hoped, his ghostly hand pushed through an iron bar as though it were only a stream of water. The rest of him followed, and he stood on the gravel drive of the Manor grounds for the first time in his life.

He strode between the weeping white spruce that lined the drive like sentries. Yorik marveled at how quietly he moved. He seemed to weigh almost nothing at all. His feet, stepping lightly, did not crunch on the gravel. He did not even need to breathe. He moved with perfect silence, one with the night. He looked up at the stately Manor and remembered the ruby knob cutting the air. He felt angry and invincible.

He heard a growl and stopped.

One of the hounds crouched on the gravel drive between Yorik and the Manor, in the shadow of a weeping spruce.

Yorik knelt and lowered his balled fist. "Here, Hatch," he said calmly. "What are you doing out of your kennel at night?" His first instinct was to return this escapee to the Kennelmaster. But why should he? He no longer served Lord Ravenby. He served the Princess, and he was certain she would not care if a few of the hounds ran loose.

Hatch did not heel. He growled a rumbling threat and showed his white teeth.

"Heel!" ordered Yorik, clicking his tongue.

Another growl, from the left. Two more hounds, Oke and Dye, padded closer on the short grass. There appeared to have been a mass break from the kennels.

Yorik rose slowly. He knew better than to show fear. He remembered what his father had taught him. *Never show fear to hounds. And never run from a pack.* This lesson had been meant for the hunting packs they sometimes encountered in the common forest, not for the hounds of Ravenby. These dogs were Yorik's friends.

But now he could see dark forms darting from the shadow of the Manor. Growls and woofs surrounded him. He heard hot, panting breaths. A whiff of burning phosphorus floated on the air.

He fixed on Hatch, the pack leader. "Hatch, boy," he called. "It's Yorik. Heel!"

Hatch ignored him. The hunting pack tightened on Yorik like a noose.

Well, thought Yorik. *Let them come. What can they do to a ghost?*

Then Hatch slid from the shadow into soft

moonlight. Yorik saw the familiar shape of the hunting hound—and something more. Hatch was enclosed in a green shine. No, not a shine, Yorik realized. An outline, an encompassing likeness of a larger Hatch, its fire eyes glowing like embers in a pit, its pale green teeth reflecting the moon. Hatch the hound was enveloped by this shape, this demon-hound, which moved with him as one. The other hounds, also bound in demon forms, crept onto the path.

Yorik fled for the gates.

The hounds did not bay as they did when they chased game. But Yorik heard the smack and hiss of flying gravel and knew they pursued. He felt as he imagined the fox feels as death closes in.

In seconds Yorik was through the gates. He turned. There was no hope in running farther. If the gate did not stop the hounds, then—he didn't know what.

The pack had stopped short of the gates. They paced and prowled behind the iron bars, watching hungrily with fiery demon eyes and growls that sent tremors through the earth.

"Come!" thundered a voice. Yorik knew that voice. It was the Kennelmaster. The hounds retreated from the gates as their master emerged from the shadows, bundled deeply in scarves, his breath puffing in clouds.

"Mr. Lucian!" called Yorik. He stepped closer to the gate, eyeing the green shapes circling ominously.

The Kennelmaster clenched the iron bars with gloved hands. He thrust his sharp nose between the bars, eyes crinkling as he peered into the dark. He did not look at Yorik.

"Mr. Lucian . . ." Yorik brought up a hand in greeting.

"D'you hear that, boys?" called Mr. Lucian softly. He relaxed his grip and turned to the hounds. "That moaning there in the shadows? 'Tis not a Dark One. 'Tis only a wee ghost. We need not fear. I'll soon drive it off."

One by one, the green glows winked out. Then all Yorik could see were the hounds, his former friends, gathered behind Mr. Lucian.

The Kennelmaster opened his battered coat. He withdrew a candle and match. He lit the candle.

The candlelight cut into Yorik. He winced and flinched back from the gates.

Hatch whimpered.

Mr. Lucian, reaching into another pocket, paused at the sound. He closed his eyes and cocked an ear. "Speak, spirit," he ordered.

"Mr. Lucian," pleaded Yorik. "It's only me, Yorik. I don't mean any harm." Even as he said it, he realized it was not true. He had meant harm indeed.

The old Kennelmaster opened one eye. "Ah," he said thoughtfully. "I cannot understand ye. Yer speech comes from the land of the dead, a far-off land, though not so far for me as for some. A man must have a foot in the worlds of both living and dead to master hounds such as these. But I ken who ye must be. Ye were my friend, were ye not? Young Yorik, who died a bad death, an unjust death."

"Yes, Mr. Lucian," said Yorik sadly. "It's me." But he understood now that his words were nothing but moans to the ears of the living.

The Kennelmaster spat on the ground. "'Tis an ugly thing, boy. Ye deserved better, and now ye seek revenge. But ye cannot be allowed inside the Manor, not in life, not in death. Know ye that yer sister is safe, given work in the kitchens by Lord Ravenby. Yer body rests in the servants' cemetery in the far field. Now ye must go and rest with it. Ye have no place here any longer."

From another pocket Mr. Lucian withdrew a small brass bell. He held the bell next to the candle.

There was something about this arrangement that Yorik did not like. "Mr. Lucian," he said desperately. "Hatch."

The Kennelmaster rang the bell.

The peal of the tiny bell was like an ax splitting Yorik's head in two. He screamed. Through a haze of pain he heard the hounds barking.

Chapter Four

Yorik ran. The Estate blurred by. He soon found himself in the water garden, halfway across the Estate from the Manor. Only here did the pealing of the little bell fade from a skull-splitting scream to a faraway whine.

He lay on his back on the mossy earth next to a decrepit stone bench, listening to the mild, eternal gurgle of the tumbling fountains, and the gentle splash of frogs and their conversational croaks. Water flowed over worn stone, and fish swam quietly in the pools.

Haunting had turned out to be much harder than the Princess had implied. He could not see how to take revenge on Master Thomas or anyone inside Ravenby Manor. And he could certainly be no help to Susan, who was trapped deep in the kitchens.

Above, the stars wheeled and revolved. Yorik's father had taught him the stars and constellations so Yorik could navigate if he were ever in a ship at sea. Naming these heavenly figures always soothed him. He spied two planets, Mercury and Vulcan, low in the east. And though Pale Moon Luna had set hours ago, he found the black disk of Dark Moon Lilith. There seemed to be more stars sprinkled about than there had been when he was alive. Orion's Belt had not had four stars in it before, Yorik was certain of that.

As he pondered that fourth star, something startling happened. The world reversed itself, and suddenly he was no longer looking up at the stars. Instead, the whole night was spread out below him, and he was viewing the stars from above.

Yorik clutched the ground as the weight of the

earth pressed down on his back and the Milky Way beckoned like an infinite river. He sensed that his tenuous grip was the only thing connecting him to the world—and that if he let go, he would fall into the universe.

I should fall, he thought. *I should let go.*

His thoughts drifted. *Yes, I should fall.* He imagined peace and ease. His grip loosened.

Yes, fall.

The stars pulled.

I am not needed here.

At this thought, his eyes flew open. *No, that isn't true,* he told himself. *I am needed here. Susan needs me.*

Fall, a voice rasped. *Here you have no place. Here you are not needed.*

"No!" exclaimed Yorik. He became aware of something on his shoulder, whispering into his ear. He swatted with one hand, and for the barest instant saw something there, or nothing, an emptiness crouching and muttering—and then it was gone.

The emptiness was gone, and the stars were back

in their proper place above him. He leapt up, his feet pressing lightly on the earth below.

Yorik reached for his weapons—his bow, his sling, his knife—before remembering they were no longer there, and would be useless if they were. He turned in a careful circle. Somewhere in the darkness beyond the starlit garden, he felt that something, more than one thing, was watching him silently, no longer whispering but waiting.

Bells and candles, demon-hounds, dark voices that came from voids—the night was fraught with danger for a mere ghost. Yorik wished that, like the stars, he were back in his proper place. He wished he were back in the cold cabin with his sister. But he was not, and he had much to report to the Princess. He hurried for the aviary glade, staying to the open paths of the Wooded Walk, one eye fixed on the shadows.

On the way, he crossed the carriage path. As he did, Lord Ravenby's great carriage loomed out of the dark and pounded past, clattering and banging. The overworked horses, coated in foaming sweat, rolled their eyes and then were gone, off toward the carriage house. Yorik wondered why the carriage was out so late, and why the horses—normally so well cared for by the stable hands—were being pushed to dangerous limits. There must be a terrible emergency of some kind. Could a Family member be ill? He hastened on, wondering.

Back in the glade, the glow of gossamer and silver soon led him to the Princess and Erde.

"You're back!" exulted the Princess. She was busily waving her twig about, weaving spells. Unseasonable blooms were popping out all over. A gray cat, hunting birds, wandered into the glade. The Princess made an emphatic flourish, and the cat shrieked, pawed the air wildly, and raced away. "Look, Erde, the ghost-boy has returned! Well, did you frighten them to pieces?"

Yorik hesitated. "No, not exactly."

"No?" said the Princess. "Well, it's not necessary. Tell me everything you learned, ghost!"

"I learned a lot, Your Highness," said Yorik eagerly. "I couldn't get into the Manor, but—"

"What?" said the Princess. "What Manor?"

"Ravenby Manor," said Yorik. "It's the center of

the Estate . . . I mean, of the lands of my human masters."

The Princess frowned, and her twig made a shower of sparks. "The center?" she said. "Why couldn't you get in?"

Yorik felt less eager. "I couldn't get past the hounds. They—"

"What hounds?" said the Princess. "Why should a few silly hounds matter to a ghost? Scare them off!"

"These aren't normal hounds, Your Majesty. They're guarding the Manor, they—"

"Guarding it? Why?"

"I don't know," said Yorik. "But perhaps if one of you could tell me how to get past them—"

"How should I know?" The Princess shrugged. "That's servants' work. You're supposed to know these things! You're supposed to be terrifying. Dogs should be scared of *you,* not the other way around."

Yorik looked desperately at Erde. She was crawling about in the dirt. It took him a moment to realize that she was following ants. She shrugged too. "Ghosts haunt," she croaked.

"But these hounds have a demon form. And their master drove me off with a bell and candle. I—"

"Enough excuses," interrupted the Princess. "This is your job and you have to do it right! I ordered you to go out and spy for me, and you come back and tell me you can't, because of what? Bells? Candles?"

"Your Majesty, even if I can't get into the Manor, there's lots more of the Estate to explore. I could—"

"Oh no," said the Princess in a most withering tone. "There might be more *candles* out there. I never knew having a ghost-servant would be this much trouble. I should have left you all broken." She pointed her twig at Yorik. "You might frighten a dog *that* way."

Yorik backed away hastily. "Your Highness, the hounds are for hunting. They normally stay in their kennels at night. But for some reason they were out patrolling the grounds. The Kennelmaster said something about Dark Ones."

"Dark Ones?" The Princess sniffed irritably, lowering her twig. "Never heard of them. Humans have a pack of stupid beliefs, don't they?"

"*Yglhfm,*" rumbled Erde suddenly. Yorik and the Princess looked at her. She was staring at them, her huge, soulful eyes brimming with muddy tears.

"Oh," said the Princess quietly. Her face fell, and her burning silver glow faded to a soft smolder. "*Them.*"

"What?" said Yorik. "Who are y . . . gl . . . ?" He tried the word but couldn't say it.

The Princess straightened. "They're nothing for servants to be concerned about." To Erde she said, "Don't you worry. If any of *them* come around *my* glade, they'll be caterpillars."

Yorik did not get the sense that Erde was completely reassured. She turned back to her ants and began weaving her skeletal fingers into complicated patterns. The whole line organized itself and began marching off to the north.

"See how far I've fallen, Erde!" the Princess fumed. "Begging good-for-nothing ghost-boys to spy for me. Me! All because I can't see a thing outside this glade."

Erde crawled to the Princess and took her hand. Mud drops plopped from her eyes.

"I only wanted to help you," said the Princess. "Curse beastly Father!"

Erde grunted sympathetically.

"Your Majesty," said Yorik. "Please, I can help. Tell me more about the Yg . . . the Dark Ones."

"*Yglhfm.*" The Princess gave a dark laugh. "You can't even say the name. I told you, they're not your concern. They involve powers you humans cannot grasp."

"Not a human," grumbled Erde.

"Close enough," snapped the Princess. "These mysteries would blast its mind into a million fragments!" She peered at Yorik. "You don't want your mind blasted into a million fragments, do you?"

"No," said Yorik.

"No, you don't," continued the Princess. "Because it's very unpleasant. So stop asking!"

Erde released the Princess's hand and went back to giving orders to the ants.

The Princess raged on. "This is all beastly Father's fault! Now I'm stuck with a useless ghost who's scared of a couple of dogs. Dogs! I could turn them all into caterpillars if only I could leave this stupid, horrible glade." Her leafy twig sparked and sputtered.

"Your Highness," said Yorik, "why does Erde need your help?"

"Just look at her!" the Princess said, pointing her twig. "They're killing her! Can't you see?"

Yorik looked with worry at small brown Erde. No one seemed to be killing her at the moment. He took a different approach. "Why can't you leave? Why did beastly Fa— I mean, why did your father trap you here?"

Everything in the glade went silent. The birds stopped chirping. The frogs stopped croaking. Storm clouds gathered on the Princess's face. Only Erde continued communing with the ants as though nothing were wrong.

Yorik felt that he had asked the wrong question. "My apologies, Your Majesty," he said quickly. "I—"

"You know," said the Princess ominously. "Having a servant ghost-boy has not worked out as well as I'd hoped. First you run away from a bell, and then you ask a lot of rude questions."

"I'm sorry," said Yorik.

"Perhaps you should go," replied the Princess coldly. "*Yglhfm* are my enemy, and there's obviously nothing *you* can do against *them*."

A black pit formed inside Yorik at these words. Then he became aware of Erde standing beside him.

"Need him," Erde said to the Princess.

"No!" shouted the Princess. "I don't need him! You are both forgetting who I am!" There was a thunderclap. She leveled her twig at Yorik. "Leave my glade," she said, seething. "Get out."

Yorik looked at Erde, whose eyes sparked grimly.

He bowed. "I'm sorry," he said. He turned and left the glade.

Chapter Five

Yorik moved back into the cold cabin.

The cold didn't bother him. Rather, he discovered that the neglected, dust-heavy, cobwebbed room suited him. Nights, he shuffled about the cabin and its environs. Days, dazzled by the sunlight, he retreated to a dim corner, where he huddled until darkness returned.

He spent seven nights in this lonely condition. He hoped that perhaps Susan might visit her old home and he would be able to see her. But of course, with her new duties at the Manor, she would not be likely to leave. His instinct was to venture out, to trap or hunt or gather, or to patch the drafty holes in the walls and thatched roof. But even if he could have done these things, there was no one for him to feed, and he had no need for shelter from cold or rain.

On the eighth night, boredom and restlessness drove him to wander farther from the cabin.

He wanted to stay away from the Manor, the servants' cemetery, and the aviary glade. And so he trudged along the Wooded Walk, past the Summerhouse, and up the Red Lion Steps. He found himself in the topiary garden. He wound along its paths, looking at the fantastic shapes sculpted skillfully from holly, myrtle, and yew. Most were animals, but there were also pyramids, obelisks, and clouds.

In the center of the well-groomed topiary garden was a large mound on which the grass grew wild. It was enclosed by an ornate little fence that no one ever crossed. Yorik recalled whispered stories that someone had been buried there long, long ago, and that the mound was perhaps haunted.

Well, thought Yorik, *if it's haunted, then whoever is*

*doing the haunting might teach me something about being
a ghost.*

He crossed the spiky fence. As he stood at the foot
of the mound, a gust of wind came up, lashing the
wild grass. The wind blew through the assemblage
of animals, tossing their branches. The cloud-
shaped pines seemed to tumble amid the animals,
which in turn seemed to leap and frolic. A laurel
lion crouched, then leapt playfully at a holly
elephant, which reared and lifted its trunk, just
missing a myrtle swan taking flight. Everything
went around the mound like Yorik imagined a
carousel might. The gust died as suddenly as it
arrived, and the carousel stopped—but now all the
animals had turned toward the mound and bowed
or lowered their heads.

Yorik turned. There, on top of the mound,
crouched a motionless hare.

Yorik automatically considered how he might
shoot the hare. But of course, that was no longer
needed. He watched the hare. The hare watched
him. Yorik ascended the mound, expecting the hare
to bounce off into the bushes at his approach.

Curiously, the animal did not flee. Instead, it regarded Yorik with glassy, bottomless eyes. Yorik stepped closer. The hare remained utterly still.

There was so much intelligence in the hare's eyes that Yorik felt compelled to speak.

"Good evening."

Good evening, replied the hare solemnly.

"Why aren't you afraid of me?" asked Yorik.

Should I be? inquired the hare.

Yorik thought about the many hares he had snared for the Manor kitchens and for his family's supper. "Hares are afraid of people."

You are not a person, said the hare.

"Then what am I?"

You are a child of the living night, as am I.

"You're dead too?" asked Yorik, as politely as one could ask that question. The dignified hare invited the utmost respect.

No, the hare replied. *Not yet.*

That answer hushed Yorik. Still the hare did not move, but gazed searchingly at him. Yorik realized that this hare was larger than it had seemed at first. In fact, it was growing.

"What are you?" said Yorik.

I am a hare, came the reply. But Yorik could see that the hare was suddenly as large as himself. No, much larger. The hare grew taller, until it towered high above him, looming like the Manor. Its fur was now a leafy tangle. The hare had become a majestic yew tree, and its eyes shone with starlight.

"You're a topiary!" exclaimed Yorik.

The topiary hare did not answer. Another gust of wind blew, but the carousel animals did not move. Yorik felt their respectful stillness in the presence of the hare.

He ventured another question. "Why is it that I have never seen you before?"

The hare's voice assumed a rich cant. *There is much you can see now that you could not see before. You can see things as they are. You can see both that which is living and that which is dead.*

"Yes," answered Yorik.

What else have you seen? inquired the hare.

Yorik thought about this. He thought about the foam-flecked horses and the whispering voice and Erde's muddy tears. "Something is wrong with the

Estate," he answered finally. "Something bad has happened."

Silence, wind, and rustling leaves. Then— *The land is being consumed by the* Yglhfm. *What shall you do?*

"Me?" asked Yorik, surprised. "There's nothing I can do."

No, Ghost. There is much of which you are capable.

This time Yorik was the one who was silent.

What shall you do? came the question once more.

"Why are you asking me?"

It is not I who asks. I ask on behalf of the Oldest, mother of us all.

"The Princess?" asked Yorik, confused. "But she told me she doesn't need me. She threw me out of her glade." He did not understand any of this. No one had ever asked Yorik to do anything. Yorik had only been ordered to do things, all his life and all his death.

"What happens if I do nothing?" he asked, genuinely interested.

I do not know, came the reply. *It is your choice.*

"I want to protect my sister," said Yorik.

Is not the fate of one bound to the fate of all?

Yorik had not thought about it that way. If the Estate was in danger, then his sister was too, and protecting the Estate would do the same for Susan. "What can I do to help, then?" he asked.

We do not know, Ghost, replied the topiary hare. *We do not know how to stop the* Yglhfm.

Yorik suddenly felt a presence—the same presence he had sensed in the water garden. He looked past the hare, past the mound, and into the woods beyond the topiary carousel. There he saw a shuffling emptiness gliding between the trees, the same emptiness that had crouched on his shoulder and rasped into his ear. He heard soft muttering.

"Is that a Dark One?" he asked.

Yes, said the hare, but its voice was strained. Yorik sensed another presence, and then another, three in all, gathered outside the topiary garden.

A tremble raced through the branches of the hare. *We must leave for now,* it said. *As must you.*

As Yorik watched, the starlight in the hare's eyes faded. He turned to the other animals. The lion, elephant, and swan were motionless, back in their places, no longer bowing toward the mound.

The muttering grew louder. *Ghost*— the dark voices began, but Yorik did not pause to listen. He raced from the garden with all the swiftness of wind.

Back in the one-room cabin, he pondered the words of the wise and dignified hare, who believed that protecting Susan would protect them all. He thought of the terrified horses, the hounds who guarded the Manor, the Princess, Erde, Master Thomas, and Susan.

Is not the fate of one bound to the fate of all?

If that was true, then he had to find a way to protect them all.

Yorik could see that the dismal cabin was falling to ruin, soon to be reclaimed by the forest. He looked at the cold ashes in the fireplace, and for a moment he could see three people there: Father, himself, and Susan, laughing and playing as a warm fire blazed.

He shook his head and turned away. That world was gone.

He walked outside, looked at the cabin for the last time, then strode off toward the Manor.

Chapter Six

As Yorik walked down the carriage path, he recalled what Mr. Lucian had said: *Ye seek revenge.* At first that had been true. But no longer.

Pale Moon Luna had set hours ago. Even with Yorik's ghost eyes, the world around him seemed sunk into a well of black. Silence was heavy over all the thousands of acres of Ravenby Estate, its four great hills, its innumerable trees. The only sounds came when he passed the mews. Inside he could hear the falcons stirring, unsettled and anxious.

Then he heard a voice.

"Yorik, dear Yorik." It was a girl's voice, high and laughing and pretty.

Yorik looked around. The voice seemed to float from a distance. Nearby there was a stone arch, with a little path of trampled dirt going under it. Yorik followed the path into a small clear space, like a bubble carved out of the dense bushes and trees. In the bubble was an old marble bench, and on the bench sat a girl.

"Mistress Doris," Yorik breathed. He automatically bowed.

Mistress Doris had been dead for years, but she had been older than Yorik when she'd died, so now they were nearly the same age. She wore one of her beautiful dresses, and had an expensive hat and perfect shoes. She patted the bench beside her and giggled. "Dear Yorik, I'm not your mistress any longer. Sit beside me."

Yorik sat awkwardly on the stone bench. "I was sorry when you died," he said haltingly.

It was true. Mistress Doris had not been a friend exactly. But she had been the terror of the Ravenby family, and part of being the terror of the

Ravenbys involved consorting with children like Yorik and Susan. She stole things from the Manor and distributed them to servants, who dutifully returned them. She broke things; she escaped at night; she fought the other noble children who came to visit. And then curiosity had gotten the better of her, and she had gone to look at plague victims, and caught the plague herself, and died.

"Well." Doris smiled. "I'm not sorry you died. Now we can have terrific fun together."

"I can't have fun," explained Yorik. "I have to protect Susan. She's working in the Manor kitchens, and—"

Mistress Doris waved her hand. "Yes, you need to protect her from my horrid brother, don't you? He murdered you, and no doubt he will gladly murder your sister too."

Yorik gaped. "I don't think—" He was not sure what to say. He didn't think Master Thomas would deliberately murder Susan. Would he?

"Yes," said Mistress Doris. "To keep your murder a secret, he might do anything. He is a horrible, bad, evil little boy. He must be punished." She giggled.

"Now we shall punish him. But first we must get past those demons that guard the Manor. Do you know how to do that, Yorik?"

"Y-yes," said Yorik, hesitant. "I think I do, now."

"Mmm," sighed Doris happily. "Then you can get me past them as well, can't you?"

Yorik was silent for a long time. He looked at Doris, who smiled beatifically.

"The hare said—" he began.

"The hare lies," Mistress Doris interrupted. "It is a demon, and so are those two creatures in the aviary glade. They must be punished along with Thomas. Now you must take me past those guardians."

"I don't think I should do that," Yorik said.

Doris's smile vanished. "Those demons are keeping you from your sister. And just look what they did to me."

She showed her ankle. In the ghostly skin, Yorik could see two throbbing bite marks, glowing angry green.

"The hounds are guarding the Manor from the Dark Ones," said Yorik.

Doris bared her teeth. "You don't have a choice, boy. I order you to take me past the demons."

Boy? Doris had never spoken to him that way before. "I don't serve Family any longer," he replied.

Mistress Doris's face went white. "You are a servant and always will be. You will get me past those demons and we will finish my naughty brother."

"No," said Yorik, confused. Doris and Thomas had fought incessantly, he remembered. But Doris would not have hurt her brother.

Doris inched closer. "You know what happened last time you disobeyed a Family command." Yorik watched her eyes cloud over and then swirl away into empty voids of deepest dark.

"Yes," he said, staring straight into the voids. "But I don't think you're really Family."

Mistress Doris scrambled up to Yorik until her furious white face was only inches from his. "Yesss," she hissed. "I'm Missstresss Dorisss."

"No, you're not," he said clearly. "I can see things as they are now. And you're not really Doris."

"Ifff I'm not Fffamily," she whispered, "then what am I?"

Yorik remembered seeing that emptiness before, in the darkness of the water garden and the trees beyond the topiaries. He looked at the glowing bite marks on Doris's ankle. "You're a Dark One," he said.

The thing gave a harsh chuckle. *Not ONE,* it rasped. *MANY.*

Mistress Doris's face became dry and hollow. The skin smeared and faded. And just before the image of the girl disappeared, those black void eyes cleared and became a girl's again, and a tiny, distant voice, the voice of Mistress Doris, pleaded, "Yorik—help me!"

Then she was gone.

In her place sat several things, or not-things, presences that were there and not there. There were more than he had sensed before—perhaps five. They were each a little blob of midnight, plump like large pears. He saw that there were a few more up in the trees, squatting on branches. They did not seem to have eyes or any other features, but Yorik sensed that all of them were looking at him, and in that look he sensed a vast, terrifying hunger.

Revenge, they chorused. Two Dark Ones dropped from a tree and slid closer to Yorik.

"No," said Yorik, leaping up.

The two stopped. *Revenge,* they said in their rasping whine. *Revenge on the one who killed you. Revenge on his family.*

"No!" said Yorik firmly, shaking his head. "No revenge."

Then we will take you, they chorused. *We will take you like we took the girl. Like we are taking her brother.* They slid toward Yorik, and despite his desire to show courage, he stepped backward. An unfamiliar panic seized him, a wild fright as he imagined the Dark Ones consuming him, and Susan's death at the hands of the evil Master Thomas.

The two nothings sprang toward his shoulders.

Then there was a terrific whoosh, and two objects flew past Yorik. They caught the nothings in midspring with a tremendous *thump.* Yorik thought it sounded like someone had punched a ball of dough. The objects sped onward, taking the Dark Ones with them.

Suddenly the vast hunger was no longer focused on him, but on something behind him.

There in the path crouched the tiny sticklike

figure of Erde. As Yorik watched, she reached her little clawlike hands into her mouth. They emerged with two dripping mud-balls. With a snapping twist of her body, she threw the mud-balls, and two more Dark Ones went flying from the bench with a magnificent *thump.*

Instantly the Dark Ones abandoned Yorik and clustered around Erde. More appeared in the trees above her. He could sense waves of ravenous hunger washing from them to her, far stronger than their craving for him. And Yorik could sense something else. He could sense their triumph.

Erde twisted and whirled, but there was no escape. She curled down and made two more mud-balls and threw them, but there were too many of the hungry voids. They pressed close to her, dropping from the trees, growing larger as they neared, as though opening their voids to devour her.

With a rushing leap, Yorik jumped over the cluster. He landed in the tiny gap between them and Erde and reached for her. He felt her long fingers wrap twice around his fist, clenching so tightly it hurt. He looked into her eyes and saw sheer and abject terror staring back from their deep brownness.

He lifted Erde into his arms and ran. The girl weighed almost nothing, and the world flashed by—carriage path, riding lane, forest, fishponds, shooting range, and then the aviary glade.

The Princess was there, in an orb of throbbing light. Her face was streaked with tears. When Yorik knelt and placed Erde on the ground, the Princess instantly gathered her into that glowing, silver, loving light.

Yorik turned. The protective light illuminated everything. There were no Dark Ones to be seen.

"Why?" the Princess was screaming. "Why did you leave? They could have destroyed you!"

Erde's voice was muffled by folds of the Princess's gossamer gown. "Looking for him," she growled.

"You can never leave again, no matter what, never never," cried the Princess angrily, sobbing. Then her eyes flashed at Yorik. "This is your fault!"

But Yorik was not looking at the Princess. He was looking toward the Manor, where Master

Thomas was, and remembering what Dark Doris had said about keeping Yorik's murder secret. Those had all been lies—hadn't they?

He left the safety of the Princess's light and raced for the Manor.

Chapter Seven

Yorik entered the Manor grounds through the limestone wall by the kennels. The piled stones had a strong, musty odor he had never noticed in life. He half expected the old stones to tumble as he pushed through, but they did not seem aware of his passing. He peeked inside the kennels, but Mr. Lucian and the hounds were not there. He hadn't thought they would be.

He walked across the frosty grass toward the hulking and massive house. He knew the hounds would come.

And they did.

He felt a presence to his left. He turned and saw Hatch watching him, enclosed in his green and glowing demon form. The hound rumbled and growled, deep in his chest.

Yorik knelt in the grass. He raised his balled fist. "Here, Hatch," he called softly.

Hatch crept closer, his paws crunching in the frost, his fire eyes burning at Yorik. His muscles were tensed to lunge.

Yorik waited.

The hound leaned toward the waiting fist. His nostrils flared, and he padded around the boy, sniffing from all sides. Yorik sat calmly, feeling the hound's bonfire breath wash through him. The green glow pulsed, and the whiff of burning phosphorus strengthened.

When he was finished, Hatch crouched on his haunches in front of Yorik and whimpered happily. The bold green tongue came out of his mouth and licked Yorik's hand.

Delighted, Yorik reached out and stroked the hound's spirit self. His hand tingled as it brushed the green fur. Hatch nuzzled him fondly with his spirit nose.

"Hello, Hatch." Yorik grinned. For one moment he felt alive again.

The other hounds arrived, running low, gathering around Yorik. They made growls, whimpers, whines, and low barks. Yorik stood up. "Yes, I know," he said. "You must go and guard the Manor from the Dark Ones." He looked up at the sleeping mansion.

The pack woofed and raced away, spirit lights shining in the night.

Yorik made for the South Wing. He did not know the Manor, but he had heard that this was where servants entered. He reasoned that the kitchens must be nearby.

He passed high, arched windows and tall walls of stone. All the doors he saw had multiple locks. Beside a set of triple-locked wooden doors in the very back of the Manor he saw a pinpoint of fire-light. As he drew near, he saw that it was Mr. Lucian, wrapped in his scarves and smoking his pipe.

The pipe lowered as Yorik approached the doors.

Mr. Lucian sniffed the night air. "Ah, I sense ye are near, young Yorik," he said quietly.

Yorik said nothing. He knew that would be useless.

"The hounds have elected to let ye pass, so ye must no longer mean harm to the Family. And ye had the good sense to know it."

"Thank you, Mr. Lucian," said Yorik, too polite not to respond, though his voice was only a moan in the night.

Mr. Lucian went on. "I must warn ye, then. There are Dark Ones inside. Some got through without me knowing, before I brought out the hounds. A few have slipped through since. Their power is in their words. Their lies can force ye to their will."

No, they can't, thought Yorik, remembering the water garden. The Dark Ones had tried to influence him, to tell him no one needed him. And they had failed. What, then, was their true power?

"Good luck to ye, lad. May ye find yer peace at last." Mr. Lucian raised his pipe once again.

Yorik pushed through the padlocked doors and into the Manor.

He wandered through the South Wing. He

walked through doors and walls. He found rooms full of beds where servants slept. Everything was dingy and musty and cold. Wallpaper peeled from walls. Carpets were worn through. Twice, Yorik thought he saw another person out of the corner of his eye, but when he turned, the person was gone. *Another ghost?* he wondered. But if there were others like him in the Manor, they were keeping to themselves. At last he found a kitchen—and Susan.

The Matron and several girls had risen early to ready the kitchens for breakfast. Several enormous stoves needed fire. Susan was at work in front of a vast field of eggs, cracking them into bowls. Beside her was bread for slicing and bushels of oranges for squeezing. All around, kitchen maids bustled.

Yorik longed to run straight to his sister. But the people, and light, and fire overwhelmed him. He shrank into a quiet, shadowed corner. His sister was singing softly; he could hear her clear voice under the kitchen din:

> Her eyes the glow-worm lend thee,
> The shooting stars attend thee;

> And the elves also,
> Whose little eyes glow
> Like the sparks of fire, befriend thee.

The Matron, passing by, put her hand on Susan's shoulder. "'Tis a beautiful song, my dear," she said. "Where did you learn it?"

Susan smiled wistfully. "My brother taught it to me, ma'am."

The Matron nodded sadly, stroked Susan's hair, then moved on.

Susan continued humming the tune as she cracked one egg after another.

Watching his sister, Yorik sang quietly:

> No will-o'-the-wisp mislight thee,
> Nor snake or slow-worm bite thee;
> But on, on thy way
> Not making a stay,
> Since ghost there's none to affright thee.

Then he saw Master Thomas.

Or rather, he saw Master Thomas's eye, peering

from a crack in a doorway far on the other end of the cavernous kitchen.

Master Thomas was watching Susan.

The crack closed.

Yorik rushed through the wall. He darted through another wall and then another, to a corridor where Master Thomas's round form was bumping up a stairway. But something about the round form was too round, too humped. Something about Master Thomas had changed.

Yorik followed.

Then Yorik realized why the form was wrong. He realized he could not get too close to Master Thomas, not yet.

He must not let the Dark Ones know he was there.

Two of their blobbish shapes squatted on Master Thomas's shoulders. Yorik could hear them making urgent, murmuring sounds. From this distance, Yorik could not tell what they were saying.

He followed as close as he dared. They were no longer in the dingy, peeling, threadbare part of the Manor. The carpets were thicker now, the floors polished. Mirrors hung on the walls. Glistening silver and paintings could be seen. Doorknobs shone.

They were climbing. Yorik crept up long, wide staircases with marble banisters, keeping Master Thomas's hurrying form ahead of him. Once, he sensed a Dark One looking back, and he leapt through a wall into a musty sitting room.

Then Master Thomas went along another corridor, turned, opened a door, and went inside.

Yorik poked his head through the wall, just enough to see into Master Thomas's lavish quarters.

Master Thomas was sitting on the edge of the bed, his hands clasped in front of him, rocking back and forth. He was crying fat tears that streaked down his face and plopped into his lap. His weeping face was torn with misery.

You must kill her, said the Dark One on Thomas's left.

She knows your secret, said the one on the right. *She knows what you did. She will tell your father.*

Then the two chorused together: *And when your father knows, he will banish you. You have always disappointed him. You are useless and weak. He wishes your sister still lived, so that the Estate could be left to her instead of you, you worthless failure.*

Master Thomas moaned.

"No," whispered Yorik.

Instantly the Dark Ones turned their hunger onto Yorik.

The ghost-boy! they chattered. *He is here!*

Yorik stepped through the wall into the bedroom. "Leave him alone," he said.

Look, they whispered to Master Thomas. *Look! The ghost of the murdered boy has come for revenge!*

Master Thomas sniffed. He blinked in confusion.

Look, fool! screamed the Dark Ones. Then they began to make noise, a high, whining, and monstrous sort of singing.

Though Yorik knew that Master Thomas was not aware of the Dark Ones on his shoulders, something about that piercing song seemed to direct the boy's attention. Master Thomas peered into the dark corner where Yorik stood.

Their eyes met. Horror sprang onto Thomas's face.

"No!" said Yorik. "Wait, the Dark Ones, they—"

But it was futile. Master Thomas leapt to his

feet. "Yorik!" he said. "No!" He stumbled backward.

Run! screamed the Dark Ones.

Master Thomas ran through a set of doors onto his balcony.

Yorik wished he had Erde with him. She could do something about the two Dark Ones. Not knowing what to do, not wanting to scare Thomas further, Yorik began to leave.

Then, through the doors, he saw that Master Thomas was standing on the stone balcony railing.

The Dark Ones screamed of ghostly terrors, of a wrathful Yorik coming to seek vengeance.

Master Thomas wobbled on the balustrade. He seemed to think he could escape by leaping to the next balcony. But Yorik could see that it was too far, and Master Thomas, never a graceful boy, was going to fall.

Yorik ran onto the balcony, wondering if somehow he could tear the Dark Ones away before something awful happened. They were hissing more whispers into Thomas's ears, urging him on with *You fool, you useless, cowardly, stupid, hated waste—you must jump!*

Yorik reached hopelessly for Thomas as the Dark Ones shrieked in triumph and vanished.

Master Thomas fell through the night.

Yorik raced to the balcony's edge and looked over.

Far, far below lay the body of Master Thomas. Yorik, having had one himself, could see that the boy had a broken neck.

Twelve-year-old Master Thomas lay on the hard, cold ground, dead.

Chapter Eight

The Princess had established herself on a sort of throne, which she had cultivated from the low branches of a sycamore.

"Hmm," she said. "A really horrible, nasty, tragic death, by the sound of things."

"Does that mean he'll wake as a ghost?" asked Yorik.

The Princess frowned. "I hope not. I've enough trouble with the ghost I've already got."

"Saved me," croaked Erde, almost angrily. She was huddled in the dirt.

"Yes," sighed the Princess. "He did. Well," she said to Yorik, "if that one does turn up, I don't want you bringing it back *here*. I've finally got the place looking respectable."

Yorik agreed that the glade looked lovely, especially in the nighttime. He was sitting on the grass in the middle of an absolute explosion of flowers, perfect green flora, and tall, thriving trees. Yorik wondered why the Princess was doing all of this in the middle of winter, but knew he could not ask. Only after he'd saved Erde had the Princess allowed him to return to the glade.

But he did have other questions.

"I don't understand why Master Thomas could see me," said Yorik. "None of the other living can."

The Princess yawned. "Probably because you're supposed to haunt him. He's the one who murdered you, you know."

Yorik had been pondering this. "I don't think he did that on purpose. Killed me, I mean."

"Let's find out," replied the Princess. She pointed her leafy twig.

A flickering, faded image appeared near the elm.

It was Master Thomas, bundled up in his white wool coat. *It's an apple tree,* said the image. *Now start climbing.*

Yorik stood, startled. "Is that a ghost?"

"Sort of," said the Princess, twirling her twig. "It's a memory."

Two flickering gray Dark Ones were hunched on the shoulders of the image. They spoke, sounding whispery and scratched. *The servant boy is very clever. He'll find out what you did. Throw a rock. Throw a rock.*

They repeated this again and again. The image bent, chose a rock, and threw it. The Princess twitched the twig, and the image vanished.

"I'd find out what he did?" said Yorik, surprised. "What were they talking about?"

"I don't know." The Princess shrugged. "But it's only human business, so it can't be very important. I have other things to worry about." She looked at Erde.

Yorik was worried about Erde too. She had dwindled since her encounter with the Dark Ones. She had stopped having conversations with ants, or drawing in the dirt. She mostly huddled, slumped and motionless.

"Are you sick?" Yorik asked.

Erde nodded. "Sick," she sniffled. A piece of mud fell from her mouth. Yorik noticed that the mud was drier than it had been. Erde was drying up, like the creek bed during a drought.

"Can't you help her?" said Yorik to the Princess.

The Princess shook her head grimly. "I *could*," she began, "but beastly Father—"

Yorik was done with hearing about beastly Father. "What does that have to do with it? The Dark Ones can't come near you. You have loads of power."

The Princess's eyelashes fluttered. "True. But my power is limited to this glade because of—"

"Beastly Father," said Yorik.

The Princess gave Yorik a withering look. "Yes. The instant any bit of me left my glade, he would know. And Erde's sickness comes from outside. It comes from *them*."

All of Yorik's attempts to repeat their word for the Dark Ones—*Yglhfm*—had only made the girls giggle nervously.

"I don't understand," said Yorik, "why they make her sick."

The Princess and Erde exchanged searching looks.

"Tell him," grunted Erde weakly.

"Are you sure?" said the Princess anxiously. "He's only a human."

Erde looked at Yorik. "Not a human."

"It's still a human," objected the Princess. "Just a dead one, that's all."

Erde wearily rumbled, "Tell him." She closed her dark brown eyes.

A wind blew through the glade. The trees and flowers stirred. Patterns flowed across the grass and across the surface of the pond. The light in the glade darkened.

"Very well," said the Princess. "I will show you who Erde is." And to Yorik's surprise, when she said that, her voice did not sound high and haughty as it usually did, but deeper and richer. It stirred and echoed in his mind. Goose bumps rose on his arms.

The Princess stood and raised her leafy twig. Her glow deepened, and her gossamer dress grew black.

"Be honored, boy," she said. "This knowledge is a gift rarely given to one of human birth."

Suddenly the pale moon flickered and vanished. An instant later it reappeared.

Yorik was no longer on the Estate. No, he was, but the land had changed. The trees and flowers were gone, and a river flowed through the glade where the pond had been. But he could see the four hills of the Estate rising up around him, four brown hills dotted with scrub.

And he was alone.

Yorik stood and walked to the nearest of the four hills, then ascended for a better view.

Below, the river twisted and wound through the hills. Yorik knew there was no river on the Estate, only a small creek that flowed in a different place. He looked at it with interest, then was surprised to see a red lion rambling along the bank.

Yorik looked toward the Manor.

There was something there, not a manor, but some other kind of structure. It was high and arched, made of stones piled one on the other. It had a raw look that the Manor did not, as though cobbled together by hand. The windows were made from colored glass.

Its front doors opened, and men came out, dressed in brown robes. They held spears.

They are hunting the red lion, Yorik realized.

"Yes," said the Princess's rich, deep voice. The voice descended from the starry sky, and from the night shadows all around, but neither the red lion, as it padded dreamily along the rushing river, nor the men in robes with their spears raised seemed to notice. "All of this happened ten thousand human years ago."

Yorik watched as the men spread out to encircle the red lion. Suddenly they rushed forward, hurling their spears. The red lion whirled around and roared a primal roar that shook the heavens.

Pale Moon Luna flickered out once more, and there was darkness.

"Wait, Your Highness!" said Yorik, anxious. "Did the lion escape?"

"You should ask Erde," sang the voice of the invisible Princess. "She was there."

"Erde was there? I didn't see her."

"Look closer, then, ghost. Erde is there always."

The pale moon reappeared.

Yorik saw the four hills. It was winter. The river was broad and frozen. Luna's white light glinted on the ice. The piled stones were gone, and in their place were solid huts built from wood and packed snow. Smoke rose from them. Though everything was cold and barren, the huts looked homey and warm.

"Do you see her?" asked the Princess.

Yorik turned in all directions, looking everywhere, but he saw only the hills, mist, and blown snow. "No."

"You are not looking."

"I am!" said Yorik.

"Further back, then," came the Princess's deep voice, like a rolling thunderstorm.

Dark, then light. This time there were no huts, no people. This time there were only tall trees covering the hills. There was no river, but a valley of ice that looked as permanent as a mountain. The hills were larger this time, and boulders jutted from them.

Yorik looked for Erde and did not see her. *I need a higher view,* he thought.

He found a jagged boulder on his hill and scrambled quickly to the top.

His gaze roamed over the ancient Estate.

"I see something," he said suddenly.

"Yes," rolled the voice of the Princess.

What he saw were the hills. But they were not hills. They were something else. They came up crookedly, the hills. Not hills. Knees, and shoulders. Boulders jutted up like bones and teeth, and the valley of ice like a mouth.

"It's Erde," breathed Yorik. "I see her."

"She is the soil of winter and summer," chanted the Princess's faraway voice. "She is the land and the bones beneath it."

Everywhere he looked now, Yorik saw Erde. He felt overwhelmed by her size and majesty.

"She is the Oldest!" he exclaimed. "She is the one who asked the hare to speak with me." He felt humbled that these great beings would ask him for anything.

"Yes," snapped the Princess's voice, and this time it was right next to him and as sharp and haughty as it had ever been. In an eyeblink, Yorik was back in the aviary glade, and the Princess was scowling at him, and Erde was huddled shivering in a tiny ball on the ground.

"Yes," she said again. "And you can imagine how bad things have gotten if any of *us* are asking *you* for help."

Yorik looked sadly at Erde. She was so small now. "What happened?"

"*Yglhfm,*" moaned Erde in a sad voice.

The Princess's twig slashed the air. "At first there was only one of them. It was there when you saw the hunt for the red lion. Back then it was only an infinitesimal shadow, and utterly beneath notice. But recently it somehow opened the way for others, and their numbers have swelled. And now, great Erde, poor Erde, is almost gone."

Yorik and the Princess looked grievously at little, huddled Erde.

"I'll stop them," vowed Yorik.

"And how do you plan to do that, little ghost-boy?" laughed the Princess. "However will you do that?"

Chapter Nine

L ord Ravenby laid his last child to rest in the
Family crypt in a grief-struck ceremony. Over
the three months that followed, Yorik explored
every corner of the Estate, listening and watching.
He explored the Manor too. He was careful to avoid
Dark Ones. But once, early on, he was nearly caught.

It was an evening when Yorik had been investi-
gating the bluebell patch on the Manor's hanging
terrace. Pushing through the flowers, Yorik felt a
sudden, strange trembling, hardly perceptible at
first. As the feeling grew, he found himself convinced

that this was all useless, that he was too weak to fight the *Yglhfm,* that he was only a mere ghost who fled from bells and candles.

The trembling became a flutter, and then a surge of panic that nearly overwhelmed him.

He had felt this surge before, he remembered— outside the mews, when he had confronted Dark Doris. He jerked his head up and spotted black voids gliding through the bluebells, coming closer.

"No," he said through his teeth. "You can't take me this way. Hatch!" he shouted. "Hatch!"—and then the hound was there, leaping onto the terrace and growling, and the voids fled.

After that, Yorik and Hatch always explored the Manor grounds together.

But Hatch could not enter the Manor itself. They tried once, when a door was left propped open. But a footman found Hatch in the hall and drove him away with curses and kicks.

Hatch whimpered when Yorik insisted on entering the Manor without him.

"I must, Hatch," Yorik said soothingly, stroking the hound's spirit ears. "I'll be careful."

Yorik always found the hound pacing nervously outside when he returned from within.

Inside the Manor, Yorik found that despite the hard work of the Kennelmaster and the hounds, more of the Dark Ones were somehow slipping through. Yorik learned to avoid bedrooms, where Dark Ones gathered at night, muttering into the ears of sleepers as though whispering into their dreams. And, despite his curiosity, he was forced to stay away from the grand sleeping chambers of Lord Ravenby, where the largest clusters of Dark Ones were found. He could only assume they were whispering into the dreams of the Lord of the Estate too, but in far greater numbers.

Yet he could not stay away from these chambers entirely, for it was there, more and more often, that he found Susan. She seemed to have graduated in the hierarchy of the Estate's servants, for now it was she who brought Lord Ravenby's tea at odd hours.

One night Yorik watched as she was stopped in the hallway by Lord Ravenby's doctor, who had two Dark Ones on his shoulders.

"Here, girl," ordered the doctor crisply, snapping

his fingers. Susan came obediently, and the doctor placed a vial on the tea tray. "This is sleep medicine, for your master's insomnia. Put two drops in his tea, just before it's served." The doctor hurried away.

Susan watched him leave, then put two drops in a plant instead. The next day, the plant was dead. After that, Susan threw away anything the doctor gave her for Lord Ravenby.

Soon Lord Ravenby was calling for her at all hours. Yorik noticed the older servants watching her, shooting resentful looks. They often had Dark Ones on their shoulders. Accidents began to happen, such as a servant spilling hot water on her, scalding her.

And the Dark Ones began to pay more attention to Susan too.

One night as she was bringing tea, she was turned away by the butler. "But I was told Lord Ravenby is asking for me," she protested. Nevertheless, she was forced to surrender the tray. As she left, Yorik noticed two Dark Ones following her. Yorik followed too, anxiously, keeping a safe distance.

Strangely, Susan did not return to the maids' quarters, but went up a back staircase instead. Soon she came to a storage closet, in which there was a ladder. Up the ladder she went, pushing open a trapdoor at the top. The Dark Ones were behind her. Yorik waited, then climbed after, fading up through the trapdoor. He found himself in a long, narrow, deserted attic, surrounded by thousands of things for which the household had no immediate need—stacks of beds, wardrobes, and mirrors stretched in all directions.

He heard a scraping sound and found Susan reaching into a space beneath a floorboard. From there she removed Eleanor—the corncob doll Yorik had made for her years before. She stroked the worn yarn of Eleanor's hair and gazed out a garret window into the night.

Yorik crouched, hidden in a wardrobe, watching.

The two Dark Ones crept near Susan. *You are all alone in the world, girl.*

Susan began humming softly.

You should have stopped him from killing your brother. Your brother's death is your fault.

With gentle fingers, Susan combed Eleanor's hair.

Yorik stood, putting a hand in his pocket. A few of Erde's mud-balls were there, made by her for his protection.

You are only a weak little girl. Your master is going to turn you out into the snow.

Yorik withdrew two mud-balls.

You should slip the poison into his drink! the dark voids hissed.

Yorik put one hand back to throw, then stopped as he saw his sister's soft smile. She continued humming as she carefully straightened Eleanor's homespun dress.

The Dark Ones bristled and pulsed. Then there were more, four more, fading in from the corners. Too many for Yorik's mud-balls. They gabbled and cried, surrounding Susan and chanting horrible fears at her. He had seen them do the same thing with Thomas, to deadly effect.

And then Susan sang. In a clear, high voice, she sang, looking out into the night. Yorik knew the song—a lament their father had taught them, an old song in a dead language from across the sea.

The Dark Ones' babbling taunts faded away. Slowly, silently, they disappeared back into the shadows.

Susan kissed Eleanor, laid her beneath the floorboard, and crept away.

Not that night, nor on any night to come, did they gain control of Susan. They failed, just as they had with Yorik in the water garden. Gradually, they gave up trying. Yorik watched, and wondered why this was.

The Dark Ones did not fail with others in the Manor. Gradually their control and their numbers increased. Yorik noticed that some of them had even stationed themselves in a scattered circle around the aviary glade.

The Princess wasn't worried. "They know better than to get too close," she sniffed from her sycamore throne. "By the way, if that other boy is coming back, it should be soon."

"Won't he be in danger?" asked Yorik, remembering what happend to Doris.

"I should say so," chuckled the Princess, chewing absently on the end of her twig. "Sounds like they possessed him once already. He's forever vulnerable now. They'd only have to touch him to get him back."

And so Yorik began to wait below the balcony where Master Thomas had fallen.

Chapter Ten

A summer breeze swirled through the courtyard. Yorik waited, crouched on the balls of his feet. Nearby, Hatch paced relentlessly, sniffing the wind.

This was the sixth night that Yorik had waited below Thomas's balcony, arriving after sunset and waiting until dawn. He found that being dead gave him patience enough to do this night after night, while Hatch stood guard.

The hound stopped pacing. He growled into the shadows.

Yorik tensed. From around a corner of the courtyard, toward the front of the Manor, electric torch beams sliced through the darkness, and voices argued.

Yorik relaxed. Whatever it was, it was the business of the living. He turned his attention back to the flagstones.

A ghost lay there, where moments ago there had been nothing.

Thomas opened his eyes.

"Welcome back," said Yorik, not quite able to keep the anger out of his voice.

Thomas attempted to sit up. His hands waved helplessly over the flagstones. "Wh—" he said thickly.

Yorik eyed the struggling boy. "It's not so bad. Just one broken neck, that's all. I broke that and more when I fell. Anyway, the Princess will fix you."

"B—" croaked Thomas. His head was stuck pointing sideways.

Yorik considered. Then he reached out, grasped Thomas's head in both hands, and gave it a tremendous *crank*. Now Thomas's head was facing forward, though still tilted at an angle, making him look as though he were thinking about the answer to a question.

"Not perfect," said Yorik. "But at least you won't have to walk crabwise."

Thomas floundered into a sitting position and bugged his eyes at Yorik. He swiveled to look at the courtyard, saw Hatch, and made a bleating noise.

"Wuff," said Hatch. His ember eyes flared. Warm brimstone scent wafted over the boys.

"N—!" said Thomas.

"Listen," said Yorik. "What's happened is that you died." He proceeded to explain as insects buzzed and chirped, a bat flew overhead, and Hatch patrolled the courtyard. He told Thomas about the Princess and Erde and the topiaries, and everything else that had happened since the day the Dark Ones had convinced Thomas to throw those rocks.

Thomas interrupted regularly, making thick, strangled noises. He quieted only when Yorik spoke of his encounter with Dark Doris.

Yorik finished solemnly. "And things have gotten worse since then. I've been leaving the glade every night, haunting the whole Estate, trying to find a way to stop the Dark Ones."

"Y—" said Thomas, then faltered. His gaze fell to the flagstones.

Yorik paused, looking at the other boy, remembering the rocks and the elm. At last he spoke. "I've forgiven you, Thomas. There was more to the story than I knew. I'm only here to take you to safety. The Princess said that once you've been possessed by the Dark Ones, you are forever vulnerable to their touch. We'll speak more later, once I've gotten you back to her for repair."

"G—" began Thomas, but Hatch interrupted. The hound went stiff and made an earth-rumbling growl, startling both boys.

"What is it?" asked Yorik.

Without another sound, Hatch raced away, his green glow shining.

"Come on," said Yorik grimly. "Dark Ones must be trying to get in. The hounds can fight them. We must get you back to the glade."

Yorik stood. Thomas just sat, his face scrunched.

"Look," said Yorik. "There's no use crying.

You're dead, and that's that. You'll get used to it soon."

But the small, round figure was inconsolable. Thomas huddled on the flagstones, weeping. His burbling cries sounded like water gurgling down a drain.

Yorik groaned. "Weren't you listening? You're not safe outside the glade."

Thomas's sobs resolved into a single sound. "Fa—" he cried. "Fa!"

Yorik calmed himself. He knew he must be patient with Thomas, who had been tormented by the Dark Ones for so long. Yorik stared into the dark, where torch beams bobbed, voices shouted, and hounds barked. "Your father," he said finally. "Lord Ravenby is strong. The Dark Ones have been unable to break him."

But since your death, he has declined. I am afraid he will not resist much longer. Yorik elected not to share this with Thomas.

"Fa—" said Thomas brokenly. He struggled to his feet.

Yorik eyed him. "It's unwise for you to see him

now. And it's too dangerous for you here. I can outrun a few Dark Ones. You can't."

Thomas wobbled, as though trying to shake his head. "Fa."

"It's unwise," repeated Yorik.

Thomas wobbled defiantly.

"Very well," said Yorik. "But you must obey everything I say."

Thomas dipped his whole upper body. "Ys."

"Follow me, then." Yorik led the way across the courtyard, aiming straight for a far wall. Thomas waddled behind.

Then the argument that Yorik had been ignoring came spilling into the courtyard. There was an eruption of howls and barks. Electric torchlight stabbed through a green spirit glow. Men in flight suits and caps ran around the corner, pursued by the hounds.

Yorik recognized Lord Ravenby's dirigible crew. One of them, the pilot, had a club. All of them had Dark Ones on their shoulders.

Advancing on them were Hatch and Oke, barking and snapping, their green spirit forms bristling and bright. The crew was shouting at them.

"Rabid dogs! Get back!" They shone their torches in the hounds' eyes.

Hatch leapt at the pilot, his spirit jaws stretching for a Dark One. The pilot swung his club and hit Hatch in the ribs with a vicious crunch. Hatch fell soundlessly, and his spirit form winked out.

Oke raced for the pilot too. But the men were fleeing now. Reaching a door, they piled through and slammed it in Oke's face. The hound sat for an instant, howling, then ran back to where Hatch lay.

"Hatch," moaned Yorik. In the distance, he could see the other hounds running. Behind them bobbed the Kennelmaster's lantern. There was nothing Yorik could do. He pushed through the Manor wall.

Thomas didn't follow.

Yorik poked his head back into the courtyard. Thomas was looking fearfully at the wall and gesturing toward a nearby door.

Yorik sighed. "You don't need to bother with those anymore. Just push through the wall. It's like swimming."

Thomas looked entirely blank.

"You can't swim?" Yorik asked.

Thomas shook his head no, wobbling his whole upper body along with it. Suppressing a groan, Yorik grasped Thomas's arm and pulled him through the wall.

Yorik led the way across the Manor, frustrated with Thomas's slow waddle. As they went, he instructed the other boy. "We must avoid the Dark Ones. Try to do as I do. This late at night, almost everyone in the Manor is asleep, so most of the Dark Ones will be with them, whispering into their dreams."

Thomas nodded, lip quivering. No doubt he understood about the whispered dreams.

At last they stopped outside an ornate double door at the end of a long hallway. The corridor was dark, but firelight flickered around the edges of the door.

"Fa—!" gurgled Thomas.

"Yes," said Yorik grimly. "He's been denying himself sleep these last few nights. You'll see."

Thomas lurched for the door, but Yorik stopped him and led him to a place where they could enter the study in a shadowed corner, opposite the fireplace and away from the burning firelight.

They faded in through the wall. Thomas whined at the sight of his father.

The once-commanding figure of the Lord of the Estate was bent forward, his shoulders slumped. His mass of dark hair had turned a scraggly gray. He wore a dressing gown that had not been washed in weeks and muttered over stacks of papers that had fallen and slipped all over his broad mahogany desk.

Amid the paper piles crouched two Dark Ones, hissing their lies.

Both your children are dead. You could not protect them. You failed as their father and now you have nothing. Nothing.

Lord Ravenby shook his head and mumbled.

The door burst open. The dirigible captain stormed in, wielding his club. His flight suit had a long, jagged tear down its front.

Lord Ravenby looked up blearily. Yorik felt Thomas shrink at the sight of the two Dark Ones hissing into the ears of the captain.

"Rabid hounds loose on the Manor grounds!" the captain shouted.

Lord Ravenby's gaze wandered, vague and confused. "My Kennelmaster told me this was necessary. I can't recall why. . . ."

A Dark One hissed something to the captain, who replied, "You should have all the hounds shot at once."

"Shot, yes," muttered Lord Ravenby. He pushed back from his desk and stood. He stumbled across the study toward the fireplace. Yorik could hardly look in that direction, as the sharp firelight burned his eyes. Then Lord Ravenby stepped in front of the fire, blocking the light. Yorik watched as the man reached for the enormous rifle above the mantel— the famous rifle that Lord Ravenby's grandfather had used to hunt mammoths a century ago, when mammoths still lived.

Lord Ravenby ran his hand along the barrel of the mammoth rifle. "Shoot the hounds." He shook his head. "I'll consider it." He turned away from the fireplace.

The Dark Ones on the captain's shoulders

continued hissing. "There is no longer any reason to ground the *Indomitable*," the captain said angrily. "She's ready for flight."

"The mechanical problems—all repaired?"

Dark whispering. "Yes," said the captain.

Yorik could see that the captain was lying. When Lord Ravenby responded, "Very well, I will leave tomorrow night," Thomas gripped Yorik's arm in terror.

The captain stormed out. Lord Ravenby hesitated, then took the mammoth rifle down from the mantel and placed it across his desk before returning to his papers.

Yorik pulled Thomas into the next room. "Come on," he said to Thomas. "You've seen him. Now I must get you to the Princess."

Thomas shook his body no.

"But you have to!" said Yorik.

His eyes rolling, Thomas shook and refused.

"Don't you understand?" said Yorik. "There is nothing you can do for your father. And the Princess can't protect you outside the glade. Do you want to end up like Doris? Consumed by the Dark Ones?"

Thomas tried to make a shrug—*I don't care.* He would not look Yorik in the eye.

"Very well," Yorik said testily. He reached into his pocket and produced two small, dryish mud-balls. "Here," he said, thrusting them at Thomas. "These are the last two that Erde was able to make. Stay hidden, but if any Dark Ones find you, hit them with these."

Looking dubious, Thomas accepted the mud-balls.

Yorik turned and faded through the wall, then raced for the aviary glade.

Chapter Eleven

More of the Dark Ones had gathered around the glade. Yorik had to run in a wide circle before he found an opening in their lines.

At first he could not find the Princess. She was not with the partridges roosting in trees. Nor was she near the elm, nor walking by the pond, nor sitting on her sycamore throne. She was not in the clearing, where the remains of last autumn's snares had long vanished.

Finally Yorik discovered her beneath a spreading cherry bough. In this quiet place, the Princess had parted the long grasses to form a cradle. Erde lay within. The Princess knelt beside the withered brown girl, gently tapping her leafy twig and making little clouds of misty water that settled over Erde's dry form.

Yorik knelt beside the cradle. Erde was so small now, curled into a ball no larger than one of her old mud-balls. She wasn't speaking, and her eyes were closed.

"Is that helping?" Yorik asked, nodding at the mist.

"No," said the Princess miserably. She stood abruptly, waving the twig across the grass stains on her gossamer dress. The stains vanished. "So where's the other ghost-boy?" she asked. "He must have appeared by now."

"He did," said Yorik. He explained about Thomas.

"Too bad," murmured the Princess. "I could have used another servant."

Yorik could tell she was trying to resume her old imperious manner. But her heart was no longer in it. Even as the aviary glade burst with life, the Estate darkened, and Erde crumbled.

Yorik stood too. "Poor Thomas," he said, looking down at Erde. "He can't do anything to help his father."

"If he's so useless," snapped the Princess, "then what did you want him so badly for?"

"I only wanted to bring him here, for protection. But now I'm not sure how I would have gotten him in. A lot of Dark Ones are surrounding your glade now, you know."

The Princess laughed darkly. "I wish a few of them would drift a little closer, but they know better, don't they?" This idea seemed to perk her up.

Yorik continued. "And there are more of them everywhere, all the time. It's getting harder for me to move around the Estate."

The Princess's dismal mood returned. "What does it matter?" she said. "Did you really think you'd find a way to defeat the *Yglhfm*? In all these nights of prowling everywhere with those dogs, you haven't, have you?"

"No," said Yorik, crestfallen. "Not yet. But I have learned something. The Dark Ones are focused on the Ravenbys. First Thomas, then his father. There must be a reason for that." As he said it, he remembered the words of the topiary hare: *Is not the fate of one bound to the fate of all?*

The Princess snorted. "You would think that. Humans think everything involves them."

"But—"

"But nothing. Don't you realize you are dealing with an ancient evil far more powerful than a few humans? Not to mention you, a stubborn little ghost-boy, not even one year old!"

Yorik turned away. "At least I'm trying."

The Princess's voice turned to icicles and venom. "Beware, ghost. I can banish you from my glade. You can spend your days among the *Yglhfm* if you like. You know very well I—"

"—can't leave the glade because of beastly Father," finished Yorik. "I know." He turned to her. The Princess's leafy twig was sparking as though it were angry too. He pointed. "What if you let me use that? I could take it with me and use its power against them."

The Princess shook her head. "Can't. It doesn't

have any power except the little I put into it. And it's part of me. It can't leave either."

"Right," said Yorik. "Just like Thomas can't leave his father."

The Princess sighed. Her glowing face looked weary, as Yorik had never seen it before.

"You know, ghost-boy," she said, "you see so many things, you think you see everything. But you don't. There are things you fail to see that are right in front of you, and you shouldn't even need ghost eyes to see them."

"Like what?" ventured Yorik cautiously.

"Like your little murderer friend. Do you think he's staying with his father because he's stupid? Do you think he doesn't fear the *Yglhfm*?"

"Why, then? Why would he stay?"

The Princess sank slowly into the grass, her gossamer dress billowing. Her glow dimmed. "Perhaps," she said quietly, "it was something he did. Something terrible. And he feels responsible for everything bad that has happened since. He won't leave his father because he doesn't believe he deserves to be fixed. And so he stays there, among the *Yglhfm,* in the dark."

"My murder," said Yorik. "He feels responsible for my murder. But I've forgiven him for that."

"I mean something really, really bad," said the Princess distantly. "An unforgivable sin."

"Your Highness, I—" Yorik stopped. The Princess was not listening, nor was she looking at him. She was sitting in the grass with downcast eyes, her face shadowed, her fingers fidgeting with her leafy twig.

Her voice was so quiet now that Yorik could hardly hear her. "Sometimes you do something," she whispered. "Something so awful you can never atone for the crime. Even if you want more than anything to help someone you love . . . there is nothing you can do."

Yorik understood now that the Princess was no longer talking about Thomas.

He looked up at the stars, thinking. These nights, the sky above most of the Estate was covered with writhing flame-blue clouds. Only here, above the aviary glade, could the stars still be seen. He watched them blink and shimmer.

He looked back at the girl sitting in the grass, her head with its laurel crown cast down, her glittering hair spilling around her. "What could you . . ." He hesitated. "What could someone have done, for their sin to be unforgivable?"

The Princess's glow vanished. The aviary glade grew dark.

Then the Princess drifted up from where she sat, rising through the cherry boughs.

Yorik climbed swiftly, following her. In his ghost form, he could climb forever and never fall. At the very top of the tree he found her sitting as before, now on the very tip of the highest branch. Yorik crouched near her, balancing on a branch no wider than his finger.

The Princess raised her arm and pointed with her leafy twig. The twig moved along the sky, across the length of the bright Milky Way, the river of stars. The white Way glowed ever brighter as the twig traced its path.

"A girl was once given charge of a river," came the Princess's hushed voice, soft and sad. "A bright, clear, shining river."

As Yorik watched, the leafy twig twisted. In the river there appeared swift black shapes, dipping and rushing in the flow, free and happy in their swimming.

"What are those?" he asked.

"They are dolphins," said the Princess. "They asked the girl to come and play with them, and swim in the waters."

"Did she?"

"At first," she said. "The girl would come to the river's edge each morning and call to them, and they would come to her and she would swim with them, up and down the river's length, from its source in mountain springs to its end, where sea winds blew over salt waters."

Yorik watched the white Way glitter and gleam. It filled with more of the dark swimmers, and the stars around them seemed to dance.

The Princess went on. "All was well, in the beginning. But in time, the girl grew bored. She became angry with her father for giving her only this river, when she thought she deserved so much more. And so she left it behind, and went to other places she thought more worthy of her. She ignored the shining river."

The stars that had seemed to dance slowed and then stopped. The happy swimming of the dark shapes changed too, becoming frantic and crowded. Something was terribly wrong, and despite himself, Yorik felt afraid. He almost did not want the Princess to continue. At last he spoke. "Go on."

"A long time passed," whispered the Princess. "Then one day, the girl remembered her river. And she returned."

She twitched her twig in a sudden slash, and the bright, clear river darkened. The swimmers disappeared.

"She had been gone for many years. In her absence, the river had become black and poisonous. When she saw what had happened, she raced to the river's edge and called to the dolphins as she always had . . . but this time they did not answer. They were all long dead. There were none of them left."

Yorik felt as though his heart would break. "Princess . . . ," he said.

The girl moved her twig, and the night sky

became itself again. She sank back through the boughs, Yorik following. He knelt next to her as she huddled on the ground.

"Now you know," she said, her voice breaking. "Now you know why Father banished me to this glade, and why I may never leave."

"But, Princess," said Yorik. "Look at all you have done. Your glade is so beautiful, and you've sheltered Erde here, and you protected the birds, and you fixed me when I was broken, and—"

The Princess's voice was harsh and ruthless. "It doesn't matter. They're dead, all dead forever, and it's my fault. It is an unforgivable sin. I deserved to be punished. Father was right."

"Princess . . . ," said Yorik. He placed a hand on her shoulder.

"DON'T TOUCH ME!" screamed the Princess. Bolts of lightning shot from her twig, and Yorik was hurled backward. The pheasants, disturbed from their roosts, flew muttering down from their trees.

The Princess sat with her face in her lap, crying brokenly. Beyond was the grassy cradle where Erde lay helpless and dying.

The Princess had done something terrible, and so had Thomas. Yorik remembered the flickering image the Princess had shown him, of the Dark Ones whispering to Thomas in the glade before he threw the rocks—*he'll find out what you did.*

He'll find out what you did. Whatever Thomas had done, it had happened before Yorik's murder.

Yorik had to find out what it was.

Chapter Twelve

Yorik found Thomas hiding in the corridor outside his father's study, where the Matron, with two Dark Ones on her shoulders, was confronting Susan.

"Girl, what are you doing with that?" the Matron snarled, pointing at the supper tray Susan carried. "It's the middle of the night."

"I made Lord Ravenby eat something," retorted Susan. "He is ill, and no one else has brought him any food."

The Matron laughed. "Do as you like. But you

shouldn't stay here, you know. You should flee the Estate with the others. Wicked ways are afoot."

"No," said Susan. "Someone must care for Lord Ravenby, whatever else might happen."

The Matron's lip curled as her Dark Ones whispered. For a moment she leaned over Susan. Then she pushed past the girl and stomped away.

Yorik slipped into the shadows behind Thomas.

"Thomas," he said, laying a hand on the boy's shoulder.

Thomas turned, startled. "Yrk!"

Susan hurried away toward the kitchens, the supper dishes clattering on the tray.

Thomas started after her. "Szz."

"No," said Yorik. "Thomas, listen. I spent weeks watching out for Susan too, just as you did before you died."

Thomas stopped and looked at Yorik.

"Yes, I saw you," said Yorik. "I'd been told you were going to murder her. But I realized that was a lie."

"Blb!"

"I followed her everywhere," said Yorik. "The

Dark Ones told her terrible things. They told her Lord Ravenby was going to turn her out into the snow, and she should slip poison into his drink."

"Glg," burbled Thomas angrily.

Yorik shook his head. "None of it worked. She is strong, like your father. Maybe even stronger."

"Fa—" croaked Thomas, lurching toward the study.

"Wait," said Yorik, grasping his arm. "Thomas, there is only one way to help them now. We have to find a way to defeat the Dark Ones. I believe you know something more about them." He gave Thomas a searching look. "I need to know what happened."

"N—!" said Thomas, shaking.

"You must tell me!" ordered Yorik sharply. "Little time remains."

Thomas shrank away.

Yorik paused, thinking of the Princess's terrible shame. "I know it's hard," he said, more gently now, releasing Thomas. "But you must tell me, for your father. And for my sister too."

Thomas nodded. His broken neck turned the

nod into an odd bow. And then, his face grim, he shuffled forward, leading Yorik along halls and down narrow stairways, into the depths of the Manor.

Down, deep down, below the servants' quarters, below the wine cellars to the cold rooms where meat was stored. Down, to unlit passages where old things lay hidden under layers of dust, to deep levels of the subterranean Manor basements where no one had set foot for years. Or so Yorik thought at first. But as the dust thickened, Yorik discerned a trail of footprints. Here in the still air of these rooms, the footprints were undisturbed.

In a dank passage at the dead end of the deepest basement was an antiquated iron door, rusted and ajar. Beside it in the churned-up dust were tools—scattered mallets, pry bars, and expired torches. Someone had recently pried open the door.

As Yorik puzzled over this, he heard sounds: hammering, the groans of protesting iron—and a boy crying. The sounds came from directly in front of him. *Dead echoes,* he realized. Echoes of what had happened here, not long ago.

Behind the door was a stone wall. On it was an inscription too old to read. Some of the stones had been smashed away, and behind them a narrow passage veered deeper down.

Yorik looked at Thomas. He could only imagine how this must have seemed to a living boy—the depths, the cold darkness, the utter silence—as he worked long, dark hours to open these sealed paths.

They moved through the stone wall and walked along the passage, followed by the dead echoes of whispers and tears and crackling torches. Soon they passed windows in the walls. The windows had bits of shattered colored glass in them.

"I saw this building before," said Yorik. "Ten thousand years ago." He told Erde's story to Thomas as they went.

Thomas, nodding, pulled Yorik farther down the passage. In an alcove, Thomas pointed to a leonine skeleton with snapped and shattered bones.

"Yes," said Yorik. "The red lion."

Nearby were shovels, and fresh earth piled around a sloping pit. At the bottom of the pit, the rocky mouth of a cave appeared. As they descended,

Yorik noticed a track where someone had slid down. There was blood too, as he imagined hands unaccustomed to labor might have bled from the punishing work of smashing and digging in the dark bowels of the earth.

At last they emerged from the cave into an immense, vaulted cavern. Yorik gasped. "A mammoth graveyard!"

Filling the cavern were the massive skeletons of creatures so large they could only have been mammoths. Yorik had heard legends of such things—mammoths burying, and mourning, their dead. This graveyard was ancient, the bones brittle. In some places the skeletons were piled atop each other, and some had fallen apart into mounds so high that their tips nearly reached the ceiling.

"Yorik, dear Yorik," sang a girl in a hollow voice.

Yorik turned. Atop a mammoth spine sat a girl in a tattered dress, her bedraggled hair falling over her face.

"Doris," he said. "It's really you."

Doris brushed her hair aside. She was gaunt and pale, her cheeks were sunken, and her eyes were

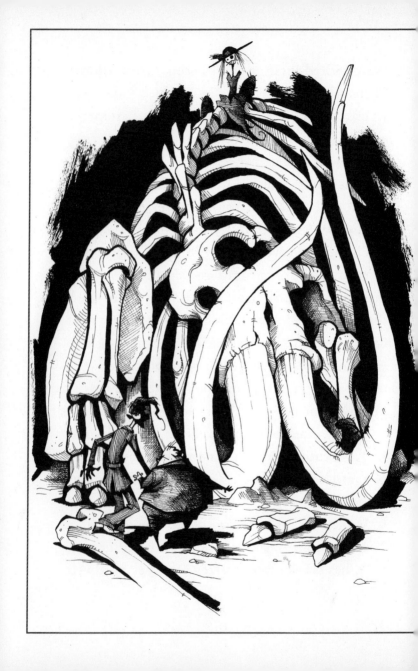

empty pits. "Yes, dear Yorik," she rasped. "But not for long."

"Ds!" shouted Thomas. He stumbled past Yorik.

"Oh, Thomas," moaned Doris. "You shouldn't have come. Neither of you should be here. The Dark Ones will return at any moment. You have to flee."

Thomas kept toward her. "You mustn't touch me," Doris said, shrinking away. "I am filled with darkness."

"Doris," said Yorik. "Tell me what happened. What did Thomas do? The Dark Ones made him open these passages, didn't they?"

Thomas stopped below his sister, moaning, ghostly tears streaking his face. "Mm s—"

Doris spoke quietly, her voice weak. "I know you're sorry, dear Thomas. I know it was hard. I saw things better after I died. I saw how Father expected of you things that you couldn't give. I saw all your sadness and pain. I wish I had been kinder to you while I lived. But now there is nothing to be done. You must run."

Yorik did not see any Dark Ones in the high,

arched cavern. But he did spy a blackness in its center. He walked closer. There was darkness here, a floating void that reminded him of a Dark One. Something was inside it. A scent wafted out, of rotting vegetation.

"Yorik, no!" said Doris in alarm.

Beside the void was an old stone tablet, broken in half. Beside the tablet was a sledgehammer. There were two runes carved into the tablet, carved so deeply that they would survive centuries, even millennia. The runes were dyed red with blood, and as Yorik studied them, he felt a warm thrill course through him. He could see that if the broken tablet were whole, it would completely cover the void.

"This tablet," Yorik said. "It blocked this portal. The Princess told me that there was only one Dark One here, until recently. Then the others found a way to come through. This is how they did it, isn't it? The single Dark One made Thomas come here and break this seal."

"Perceptive, Yorik," said Doris softly. "Our ancestors made this seal long ago, and our family has guarded it for millennia. Over the long centuries, we forgot our duty. Now my father is the only thing holding back the horde, though he is unaware of the true depths of the struggle. But his will is fading. You have only moments left. Please take my brother and run."

"Can I repair the seal?" asked Yorik. His ghost hands passed through the stone, tingling as they did.

"No, Yorik, you can't," replied Doris. "And your time is gone." Behind Doris, Yorik could hear Thomas's burbling cries.

Yorik thrust his head into the portal. Doris screamed.

A warm stench blew over him as he blinked in a sudden wash of raw blue light. Confused at first by what he saw, the images slowly came into focus. All around him, for what seemed like thousands of miles, was a vast blue expanse. The light was not blue like the sky, but blue like the color of cold flame. Floating everywhere were rich green masses, stinking like rotting plants dug up from loamy earth. And there were Dark Ones, millions of them, numbers beyond counting. Some were small like the ones he had already seen, and some were as immense as mountains or moons.

Yorik pulled his head from the opening and turned. "Doris," he began.

But Doris was no longer there. In her place stood Dark Doris, the girl he had met on the stone bench, the girl with the beautiful dress and expensive hat and perfect shoes. The girl with the proud laugh and flashing eyes, behind which Yorik could now see lurked the *Yglhfm*.

And behind her, filling the mammoth graveyard, perched on ribs and skulls and spines, were countless *Yglhfm,* thoroughly blocking the passage out.

This land was once ours, said Dark Doris. *Now we will possess her again.*

"She is dying," said Yorik. "If Erde is dead, you can't possess her."

Dark Doris chuckled. *She is not dying. She is only returning to our service. Now you will serve us as well. Come, Yorik.*

Dark Doris drifted raggedly toward Yorik, her body dragging like a marionette on a string.

Yorik backed away. But there was nowhere to go. The *Yglhfm* were everywhere.

Then Thomas, crying, waddled toward his sister.

"Ds!" he cried. "Ds!"

"No, Thomas!" shouted Yorik. "Don't touch her. You can't—"

Thomas grabbed his sister's shoulders.

Blue flame coursed over him, and he staggered. When he straightened, his neck cracked into place and his eyes flashed with the cruel, angry look Yorik had last seen when a large rock came hurtling at him in the elm.

Yorik, said Master Thomas. *It is time.*

Chapter Thirteen

A wave of chittering laughter swept over the *Yglhfm* horde. As Yorik listened, he felt a tremor in the air, and a lambent blue light flickered through the cavern.

Come, Yorik, said Master Thomas, sweeping forward. *Lord Ravenby has broken at last. Everything changes now.*

Dark Doris approached too, murmuring sweetly, her teeth bared in a maniacal smile. She and her brother glistened with new strength. The darkness beyond, full of Dark Ones, was deepening. There were more and more of them each moment, the floor of the cavern slowly filling like a pond in a downpour.

Dark Doris reached her small white hands for his.

Then Yorik spotted a faint red glow, a space on the floor of the cavern where there were no *Yglhfm*. The broken stone tablet lay there.

With a leap, Yorik was astride the tablet, one foot on each broken half. Power tingled in his feet.

Master Thomas chuckled, then cleared his throat. When he spoke, he sounded almost human again. "Give in, will you, Yorik? My father has. Let us take back what is ours."

"Erde isn't yours," said Yorik. "And you're not Thomas."

Dark Doris's pretty laugh echoed through the cavern, piercing the sea of *Yglhfm* whispers. "Oh, dear Yorik. Erde was ours for many millennia, more than you can imagine. Long before the humans came and spoiled things. For ten thousand years, we longed to draw her back into us, to embrace her, to drain and diminish her, to bring her back into bondage." She licked her lips. "And now we have."

"You can't take her completely," said Yorik, his eyes casting about for a means of escape. "You're still scared of the Princess."

"Dear Yorik," sighed Dark Doris. "Our masters have nothing to fear anymore. Look!"

She gestured to the portal. Yorik saw that it was no longer small enough to be blocked by the tablet. Now it dwarfed even the mammoths. With faint *pop*s, giant *Yglhfm* were bubbling out, one after another. Ignoring Yorik, they rumbled toward the cavern entrance, stretching to fill it completely with their vast bodies, squeezing up toward the surface.

Thousands more of the tiny *Yglhfm* surged around them. The cavern was filling, pools of Dark Ones flowing in swift currents all around the tablet but never close enough to touch it. He felt their hunger grasping for him, as it had outside the mews. And as before, he felt a crawling sensation of panic and fear. His head filled with nightmare images of Erde enslaved by the *Yglhfm,* her defenders lying dead around her.

No, Yorik thought. *It's them. The Dark Ones do this.* He concentrated on Susan and the clear lament she'd sung in the attic. He hummed a few bars, and the nightmares receded.

Master Thomas growled and edged closer, grimacing as he eyed the tablet.

"Yorik," he began—but Yorik darted forward with ghostly speed, his right hand flashing into Thomas's pocket. Then he was back on the tablet. He opened his hand and revealed Erde's last two mud-balls.

Master Thomas hissed and spat.

"I wanted these back," said Yorik.

Dark Doris laughed like tinkling glass. "Yorik, Yorik, poor little ghost. Two muddy bits against a million *Yglhfm*? Now that Lord Ravenby has succumbed, we can consume you quite easily, you know. Why don't you come and take my hand?" As she reached toward Yorik, she began to change. Her face hollowed, her eyes became voids, and her skin smeared and faded. Master Thomas, too, seemed to be melting.

You will ssserve usss, they hissed, reaching out with their spindly arms, the remains of their flesh blackening and burning.

"I'm not anyone's servant any longer, ever again," said Yorik, and he jumped.

He clung with one hand to a mammoth's rib jutting several feet over his head. *Yglhfm* pooled around Doris and Thomas, then boiled up into a mound, bearing them regally upward.

Yorik mounted the rib, then slid down to the mammoth's spine, but *Yglhfm* were flowing onto that too. He leapt to the next skeleton and the next as *Yglhfm* tumbled after him. He spied a pile of mangled and broken bones with another skeleton lying on top of it, the highest point in the cavern, its ribs poking up toward the ceiling. In three swift, vaulting leaps, he landed on the pile. All around him the dark tide rose, lapping at his feet as he ran to the final skeleton and climbed its last rib.

A cluster of small *Yglhfm* blocked his path.

Ghost . . . , they began, their formless mouths gaping.

A mud-ball struck the cluster, bowling them aside. They fell into the swirling pools below. Yorik heard children's laughter behind him.

At the tip of the rib, Yorik leapt, his hands thrusting into the stone ceiling. *Like swimming,* he reminded himself, hoping. And it worked—up and up he went, swimming into the stone, swimming up as fast as he could, the chaos of the cavern passing into silence as stone became dirt. He swam until his fingers broke into clear air and he emerged from the grass under the light of Pale Moon Luna.

He pushed himself up onto the Manor lawn, which was crawling with tiny Dark Ones.

Oke and Dye raced by in their green spirit forms, snarling and biting, seizing one Dark One after another in their teeth and ripping them to wisps. But there were far too many now, and Yorik knew the valiant hounds had no hope of fighting the enormous *Yglhfm* rumbling up from below the Manor.

He heard crashes and shouts from the Estate's far meadow. Turning as he raced across the lawn, he saw the black shadow of the *Indomitable* against the flame-blue clouds. The dirigible's cabin was half lit, and the ship was listing nose down away from its mooring tower, crewmen hanging from dangling ropes. It swerved against the dock, and the gangplank fell, crashing into the meadow, followed by splintered beams from the tower.

Yorik sprinted toward the aviary glade, evading the dark voids gliding everywhere. He dodged through the forest and along the wooded paths. Horses were running free, and shots could be heard, along with the screams of men and women. The deadly pale light of small fires sprang up all around.

As he neared the glade, he glimpsed through the trees what looked like a wall. It blocked his way, and he was forced to stop before it, puzzled. The wall was broad and made of nothing at all, and for an instant he felt again as though he were gazing into the black void of the universe. He reached for it, and his hand grew cold. He pulled back. He could see what this was now—a blockade of *Yglhfm,* thousands of them having joined the wide circle around the glade. They were piling up as he watched, already nearly up to his shoulders. This time there was no opening in the line. He gauged the height carefully. He thought he had jumped at least that high in the mammoth graveyard—an apparent advantage of weighing almost nothing. He raced back, turned, and charged the darkness, leaping up and over and landing within the safety of the glade.

He found the Princess sprawled facedown beside the grass cradle. Erde had dwindled to the size of an acorn at the bottom of her bed.

"Princess, Princess," he said, shaking her shoulder. "You have to get up!"

The Princess raised her tear-streaked face to look blearily at Yorik. "No," she said. Her face plopped back onto the grass.

"Please," begged Yorik. "I know what Thomas did. I know how the Dark Ones managed to return. There's a portal under the Manor. It had been sealed with a tablet, but the Dark Ones made Thomas break it. The tablet had runes on it. I think they had the red lion's blood in them—"

The Princess lifted her head again and sniffed. "Runes? What runes?"

"I don't know, I've never seen them before—"

"Draw them," ordered the Princess. She waved her leafy twig, and a patch of dirt appeared on the grass.

Yorik used his finger to draw what he had seen on the tablet. His whole hand tingled as he drew.

"Hmph," the Princess said, sitting up. "That's a powerful spell. Humans did that? I'm impressed. Those were the old humans, though. These new ones are worthless." She gestured toward the world generally.

"Can the runes help? Can I fight the Dark Ones with them?"

"Too late," the Princess said. "And anyway, you'd need a new lion, and . . . oh, it's completely beyond your capacity to understand."

"Then *you* have to fight them," said Yorik. "You have to leave the glade and fight them! You'd only be doing it to save Erde. Your father would forgive you."

Her eyes filled with silver tears. "No, he wouldn't," she croaked. "You don't understand. Gods don't think like humans. I can't defy him!" The Princess dropped her twig and threw herself into the dirt, sobbing again.

Yorik was about to reply when he was interrupted by a rackety, droning sound in the sky overhead.

He looked up. The *Indomitable* loomed directly above.

The rackety sound was wrong. The dirigible normally purred as it prowled the sky, flying straight and proud in the service of Lord Ravenby and his guests. Now it careened over the trees, and Yorik could see people running through the cabin brandishing weapons. Flame burst from an engine, and then the ship disappeared from view.

Yorik stood, counting the seconds. *Susan,* he thought. Lord Ravenby's last loyal servant would surely be on board.

Even the Princess had looked up from her sobbing. "Now that is the most ridiculous way to travel I have ever—"

The aviary glade shook with the power of a massive explosion.

The speed and direction of the dirigible told Yorik the terrible news. "The topiary garden," he said to the Princess, and then he was running.

Chapter Fourteen

The dark blockade around the glade was becoming taller. Yorik barely cleared it with his leap, the tips of his toes growing cold as they brushed the void.

"Yorik!"

A cry on the Wooded Walk slowed him. The Matron held a blazing torch and was stumbling through the dark, her dress muddy. She was staring at him with wild eyes. There were no *Yglhfm* on her shoulders.

No, it's a Dark One trick, he thought. *The Matron can't see me.* He ran on.

"Yorik!" another voice thundered. This time Yorik stopped.

The Kennelmaster was striding along with torch and shotgun. Beside him was Oke, limping and bloody.

"Can you see me?" asked Yorik, astonished.

"Aye," replied the Kennelmaster. "The Dark Ones are victorious. The worlds of man and spirit are joined."

"No," said Yorik desperately. "There's still time."

Mr. Lucian spat. "Perhaps a bit o' time, to flee. But too many have flooded in from the outside. We can fight them no longer."

"But they didn't come from outside—they came from within. From beneath the Manor."

"Ah, then I was wrong all along." The old man slumped wearily. "Ye fought yer best battle, I know, lad. Run while ye can." He went forward with Oke at his side.

"Where are the others?" called Yorik after him. "The other hounds?"

"Dead," came the reply. "They shot them all."

Then Mr. Lucian and Oke disappeared around a bend in the path.

"No," Yorik pleaded. *No no no.* He ran for the topiary garden.

He found the topiaries burning, each of them—lion, elephant, swan, even the great hare—a pillar of flame. The garden was sundered by an enormous furrow of earth where the *Indomitable*'s cabin had struck and slid through. In the forest beyond the garden, the airship's envelope was ablaze, billowing free from its steel skeleton. Flames from the burning engine were spreading.

In the smoke and firelit shadows, a human figure crawled from a smashed cabin window.

Lord Ravenby.

Two dark things were with him—not *Yglhfm,* Yorik saw, but a pair of shadows in the shape of children. Each shadow held one of Lord Ravenby's arms and helped him stagger away from the wreck. In one hand, Lord Ravenby held his mammoth rifle.

Behind him, the engine exploded, and Lord Ravenby was thrown forward onto the grass, the mammoth rifle clattering away.

Yorik recognized the two shadows.

"Doris," he said. "Thomas."

The Thomas shadow looked at him. *yorik,* came a scratched, tiny whisper, though the shadow had no mouth. *i'm sorry.*

"What happened?" asked Yorik.

yorik, moaned the Doris shadow. *the* yglhfm *don't need us any longer. they've abandoned us. won't you run, yorik, at last? there is nothing left.*

She pointed, and Yorik looked. There was the Manor, or what had been the Manor. Now, even as he watched, it was transforming into a mountain, the many giant *Yglhfm* piling up into a single vast, dark presence, its peak breaking above the flame-blue clouds.

Yorik turned away. "If there is nothing left, Doris," he said gently, "then why are you still helping your father?"

As if in answer, Lord Ravenby moaned and stirred, and his shadow-children floated to him and helped him rise.

Then he spotted Yorik and cried out, his eyes crazed and panicked. He crawled forward and grasped his rifle. He swung it wildly, seeming to see enemies all around. Apparently mistaking a topiary bear for the real thing, he fired.

The bear exploded in a cracking cloud, and the bullet smashed through the garden behind.

Yorik heard animal screams.

He watched the shadow-children trying to calm their father. He thought of the Princess, tending to the dwindling Erde. And thinking of the Princess, he remembered something he had seen, just before the crash of the *Indomitable*. One last chance. But he would have to move as fast as he could, as fast as a ghost could ever move, swifter than a deer, quicker than an eyeblink, for he was about to do the most dangerous thing he had ever done.

Just before leaving, he paused as a movement in the wreckage caught his eye—behind a blackened window there was a toss of hair, a frightened face, and two hands pressed against the glass.

Susan. Yorik longed to run to her. He could see she was unhurt and safe for the moment, and he knew this was likely his last chance to speak with his sister, ever again.

But there wasn't time. Gathering himself, he raced back toward the aviary glade, hurdling the blockade once more, the chill reaching into his ankles.

Fast as he was, events around him crawled slowly by. There, under the cherry boughs, crouched the crying Princess, huddled over the last dusty crumbs of Erde in the grass cradle. A teardrop hovered between the girls. In that instant, the Princess did not yet see Yorik.

Beside her, glowing in the grass where in her anguish she had dropped it, was the leafy twig.

Yorik aimed for the twig. He put his fingers down as he passed.

The Princess opened her mouth and began to turn.

Yorik snatched the leafy twig.

He had grasped a lightning bolt in his hand. His teeth seemed to shatter from the shock. But he held on, running. Something was happening behind him as he left the glade—a tidal wave of light and power. On the edge of his vision he saw curls of blistering light reaching for him like fingers.

Then he was leaping out of the glade and back onto the Wooded Walk. He had been in the glade for less than a second.

The instant any bit of me left my glade, he would know, the Princess had said.

The pain in his hand burrowed up his arm, feeling like flesh peeling away as electricity and fire ate into him.

It's part of me. It can't leave either.

He ran toward the topiary, his arm burning, electric shocks rattling his teeth. Finally the pain became unbearable, and he screamed as he dropped the leafy twig on the wooded path.

Beastly Father.

The twig danced on the ground, spitting sparks.

Yorik gaped at the space where his right hand had been. His ghostly forearm faded away into nothing. His wrist and hand were gone.

A rumbling tremor passed through the earth beneath him.

In the forest, something moved.

First he saw vines snaking from the forest onto the path and curling around themselves to form

a chair. No, Yorik realized as the shape grew—
a throne.

In the dirt at the foot of the throne, shoots appeared. Quickly they grew into tiny seedlings, then saplings. The trunks twisted into angles and put out branches, and ivy sprang up and threaded around them, forming ropy sinews of muscle around the sapling bones, until a man was sitting on the throne. Two lilies blossomed on his face, and they opened, the petals like eyelashes. And then the light from Pale Moon Luna changed, and suddenly Yorik could see each mote of dust in the air around him, the dirt and smoke from the fire suspended in the glow.

He fell to his knees before beastly Father. Warm currents of light flowed through Yorik. He opened his mouth but found he could not speak. His tongue felt paralyzed.

Beastly Father leaned forward on his throne. His lily eyes cast their filaments down at the spinning, sparking twig. He reached forth with a woody hand. As he did, the leafy twig stopped dancing and flew to him. He held the twig before his face, and

as he did so, a terrible expression of limitless anger passed over his sylvan features.

Yorik thought of the Princess, sobbing over Erde in the glade. He found his tongue. "Please, sir," he began. "Your daughter is so very sorry. She—"

The woody fingers twitched, and the leafy twig burst into flame, burning down to a cinder and disintegrating. Beastly Father's face darkened.

Yorik stood, holding out his only hand in supplication. "Sir," he said, struggling to find the words he needed. "Your Majesty . . . I know your daughter's mistake was terrible. But she has changed. When I met her she was so . . . rude. . . ." He hesitated. "Well . . . she still is. But she has become the guardian of Erde, the Oldest of this land . . . and she has protected her so fiercely against the most evil . . ."

Yorik faltered. Beastly Father was ignoring him, his lily eyes scanning the forest.

Yorik quivered. The air around him throbbed with beastly Father's fury. But he thought of dwindling Erde and dead Hatch, the sobbing Princess and the burning hare—everyone who had tried to fight the *Yglhfm* and failed.

Steeling himself, Yorik stepped forward and grasped the arm of the ivy throne. "Your Majesty!" he shouted. "You must listen to me!"

"YOU!" a voice bellowed.

Yorik whirled. Lord Ravenby was tottering down the path, his shadow-children trying to pull him back. His mammoth rifle was leveled at Yorik.

No, Yorik realized. At beastly Father.

"They told me," babbled Lord Ravenby. "They told me you would bring destruction to my Estate . . . the dark voices told me. . . ."

He fired.

The recoil blasted Lord Ravenby onto his back. Yorik heard a wet smacking sound, and turned to see a jagged hole the size of a pumpkin punched in beastly Father's chest.

Beastly Father did not seem the least concerned. But Lord Ravenby had succeeded in capturing his attention. Yorik watched as the lily filaments flickered between Lord Ravenby and his shadow-children, who were bent over their father, their hands fluttering over him desperately. At this sight, beastly Father's face seemed to soften.

He reached out his sapling arm and gestured, and the frantic look in Lord Ravenby's eyes passed away, replaced by quiet and peace. Lord Ravenby closed his eyes and slept.

Yorik seized the moment. "Your Majesty," he said. "I pray for grace for your daughter. Look toward her aviary glade and see all that she has done."

Beastly Father did not look to the glade. He looked at Yorik, his lilies wide and smoldering, the filaments aglow. For an instant they stared each other full in the face.

And then Yorik saw something high in the night sky above beastly Father. At first he thought it was Dark Moon Lilith, but it was moving, and growing larger by the moment.

"Your Majesty, get up!" he cried, scrabbling at the ivy throne, not daring to touch him. But beastly Father did not get up; he only gazed at Yorik, who flung himself away from the throne and ran as the vast *Yglhfm* thundered down from the sky. He turned to see the *Yglhfm* strike beastly Father with the force of a falling star.

Beastly Father shattered into nothing, saplings

splintered into fragments, vines crushed to pulp. The *Yglhfm* towered high above, and though its formless face and shapeless mouth had no human features, Yorik had the impression that in its own way it was gloating in victory.

Chapter Fifteen

Yorik sped back toward the aviary glade, preparing to jump. But the blockade was now taller than the trees, and he could not leap over it. Reaching into his pocket for Erde's final mud-ball, he reared back and threw, and where the mud struck the Dark Ones, there was a rippling dilation. A tunnel formed, and Yorik dove through it. The tunnel closed behind him. The mud-ball was gone. Now he was trapped in the glade too.

The Princess manifested before him, radiating white-hot fury.

Yorik spoke fast, before he could be disintegrated or imprisoned in an acorn or subjected to any of the other horrible punishments the Princess had invented.

"I saw bea— I saw your father."

The Princess dropped her hands, which, twigless, had been raised in threatening claws. The fury on her face drained into shock. "You what?"

"I saw your father. I talked to him."

The Princess seized his remaining hand. "What did he say? Did he talk about me?"

"No," said Yorik. "He didn't talk at all. Listen, there is something I have to tell you. Your father did appear, on a throne of vines, and . . . and Lord Ravenby shot him. And then a giant Dark One crushed him. Your father is dead, Princess. I'm sorry."

"A throne of vines, eh?" chuckled the Princess. "Oh, very good, Father."

Yorik looked up at the clear night sky. Here in the quiet glade, he could almost pretend that the horrors outside weren't real. "Princess," he said quietly. "The *Yg— They* have nearly won. The last few defenders of the Estate are dead or fleeing. And the Dark Ones have completely surrounded you."

"Have they?" The Princess sniffed. "They must want my glade. Well, they can crouch there eternally if they like, they'll never get it."

"Is Erde—" Yorik hesitated, not wanting to say it.

Silently, the Princess led him to the grass cradle. There in the very bottom was a crumble of dirt, falling to pieces grain by grain as they watched.

"There was nothing I could do," the Princess said in a sad, hushed voice. "Maybe I'm not all-powerful after all."

"No," replied Yorik. "But there is still something you can do. You can leave the glade and fight the Dark Ones. Before he . . . before he died, I think your father forgave you."

"You *think*? Did he say so?"

"No," said Yorik, "but the look on his face—"

"Oh, the *look* on his *face*," said the Princess with a bitter laugh. "I'm afraid you don't just zip around defying the gods, tra la la, you know. It leads to all kinds of unintended consequences."

Yorik squeezed her hand. "Princess, you have to try. The way he watched Lord Ravenby's children tending to him—"

"The who tending to what?" the Princess snapped, yanking her hand away. "Don't grab me like that, it's very rude."

"I could just tell," continued Yorik, irritated. Then he saw the Princess's eyes filling with tears. "I know it's difficult," he said more gently. "But you have to leave now. It's over. You're forgiven."

"You could really tell?" the Princess asked, her voice cracking, the tears flowing once more.

"Yes, I could," said Yorik. "Because I forgave someone too." He held out his one hand. "Come with me."

"But . . . what if you're wrong?" The Princess backed away. "You don't know what he could do . . . you're just a ghost, you can't possibly know. . . ." Yorik could see she was genuinely terrified.

"Princess, you can burn me or shock me or whatever you like, but it's time for you to leave the glade." Gently, he reached for her hand.

The Princess did not burn him or shock him, but

she did punch him weakly in the chest. "No! You don't understand! You can't understand!" She sank to her knees in the grass, her silver glow dimming to nothing. In a whisper, she said, "What I did—it was unforgivable. I can't be forgiven, ever."

Yorik watched her curiously. There was something familiar in her voice—he looked into her gleaming eyes and saw terror there, true panic and fear.

Yorik burst out in a laugh.

The Princess's head shot up. She looked at Yorik with pure poison. "Are you laughing at me?" she asked.

"Yes," said Yorik, smiling. He knelt beside her. "I just realized something, Princess."

"Well, out with it," she ordered. "Stop being so mysterious. And get that smile off your face."

Yorik composed himself. "Princess, we've been assuming all along that the Dark Ones couldn't affect you—couldn't harm you. They—"

"Of course they can't!" interrupted the Princess, sitting up. "It's quite rude to suggest! You'd better apol—"

Yorik broke in. "Princess, listen for once. We don't have much time. Do you recall the memory you showed me, where the Dark Ones told Thomas to throw a rock?"

"That other ghost-boy," said the Princess. "Of course I remember. Stop wasting time!"

Quickly, Yorik continued. He told her of the Dark Ones at the water garden, who told him he wasn't needed, and of the terrible lies he'd heard them tell Thomas in his bedroom, and Susan in the attic, and Lord Ravenby in his study. "I've always wondered," he said, "why they could influence Thomas and Lord Ravenby, and so many others in the Estate—but they couldn't seduce me into falling when I was lying in the water garden, and they couldn't make Susan poison Lord Ravenby. It's because we didn't believe their lies."

"But what does this have to do with *me*?" the Princess fumed.

"It's about the lies. They only have power over you if they are lies you were already telling yourself. The Dark Ones seduce us with our own darkest thoughts."

"And . . . ?"

"And that's why they are surrounding the glade. They're bringing all their power to bear, Princess, the same power I felt when they surrounded me outside the mews. They're pushing their lies on you, encouraging you to believe your worst fear—that you are unforgivable."

The Princess's face bloomed like a lily. "My goodness. You are absolutely right. How embarrassing." She jumped to her feet and snapped her fingers, and her silver glow returned in a burst that left Yorik blinking. From outside the glade he heard a furious roaring.

"That's over with, then," the Princess announced. "I feel terribly silly. That never would have happened, you know, if I'd been able to see out of—"

"I know, I know," Yorik assured her. "Are you ready to leave?"

"Yes," the Princess said. "I believe I am."

"Then let's go," said Yorik, taking her hand. Together they walked out of the aviary glade.

The wall of Dark Ones had vanished. Yorik led the Princess toward the Wooded Walk. With small gestures, the Princess extinguished the little fires burning here and there. A wild-eyed horse hobbled past, its foreleg broken. The Princess spoke a soothing word and the leg straightened, the horse cantering away. Then a dirigible crewman crashed from the bushes, firing his pistol at them. The Princess did not seem to notice, but Yorik watched as the bullets became honeybees and the crewman slumped to the ground, snoring.

In this way, they soon arrived at the path. The Princess released Yorik's hand. "Where is he?" she said. "I've got to go to him, you know. He can't come to me. It wouldn't be proper."

Yorik decided not to remind her of the massive *Yglhfm* who had destroyed her father. He could hear a distant rumbling from the direction of the Manor. "I don't know, Princess, but we have to move quickly." Yorik took her hand again and hurried her to the Manor lawn.

They were only steps onto the grass when Yorik noticed a firefly hovering motionless, its abdomen alight. He looked around. The world had stopped. There were motes of soot and dust and fire suspended in warm light, just as they had been a few minutes ago. He felt bathed in a spirit of purest love, and when he looked at the Princess, he saw that she felt it too. Her hand slipped from his and she rose into the air, eyes closed, as though lifted by an invisible hand. Her gossamer dress and face shone, her silver hair glistened, and her laurel crown sprouted white flowers. As if from far away, Yorik heard the faltering voice of the young Princess and the warm, rich voice of her gentle father. They were speaking in a beautiful language that he could not understand. There were tears in the voice of the girl, but happy tears now, and happiness in the stern tones of her father too.

Of course he's not dead, thought Yorik, feeling embarrassed that he had ever thought her father could be disposed of so easily.

Then time began again. The Princess drifted back to the ground as the dust motes swirled away in a sudden burst of foul wind. They were on the Manor lawn under a bloody sky, distant screams all around, and a *Yglhfm* mountain towering over them, so tall now that Yorik could not see its peak.

A furious roar shook the heavens. Violent blue thunderbolts slashed the clouds.

The Princess was beaming. "Ah," she said. "At last I'm my old self."

Yorik pointed upward. "Princess, it's time. You must fight the Dark Ones. They've all combined together somehow to form this mountain, and—"

"Oh, Yorik," said the Princess, her face tear-streaked and dreamy. "Isn't it wonderful? Father has forgiven me. I'm free."

"I know," said Yorik. "Now, Princess—"

"And I owe it all to you," the Princess continued in a misty voice. She clasped his arm. "Lovely, lovely Yorik. My little ghost friend."

Yorik grasped the Princess by the collar. "Dark Ones! Millions of them, they—"

But he could see the Princess was not at all focused on the immediate problem. Around them the grass was putrefying, stinking like the rotting vegetation in the Dark Ones' world. Yorik could no longer recognize features of the Estate, and here and there masses of earth were pushing up into new hills.

"Yorik! Oh no, your arm!" The Princess's face creased in deep concern. "Dear Yorik, what happened to your little arm?"

"Your twig fried it off. Princess, look!" He tried to turn her by the shoulder.

"Oh yes," said the Princess vaguely. "My leafy twig." She looked at her hand. "Where is it?" She knelt and began feeling around in the grass.

"Your father burned it to a cinder," explained Yorik quickly. "Princess, please—"

A dark chorus of angry bellows interrupted. Yorik looked up. The mountain was now ringed by foothills, which surrounded him and the Princess as though they were at the bottom of a vast bowl. Atop each hill were crowds of giant *Yglhfm.* They began crashing in black waves down toward the center. Thousands more were raining from the flame-blue clouds.

"He burned it?" murmured the Princess. "Oh, naughty Father . . . I must make a new one . . . let's go back to my aviary glade and get a twig. . . ." She wandered off dreamily in the other direction.

"Erde!" Yorik shouted desperately. "Princess,

remember Erde—these are the ones who hurt Erde!"

The Princess snapped to attention. She quivered as her brilliant glow turned red. "They hurt Erde," she said in a deadly tone.

She put out one hand. From the ground, a twig flew to her. Instantly it sprouted leaves. "Where are they?"

"Ah . . . !" Yorik swept his arm toward the on-rushing horde of *Yglhfm*.

From the dark wave, a multitude of voices combined to thunder in victory. *YOU WILL SERVE US!*

The Princess looked crossly at the horde. "Oh, you're still here? Don't you ever give up?"

She pointed her leafy twig.

"Caterpillars! All of you! Now!"

Chapter Sixteen

Yorik felt as though he had looked into the sun. He blinked until his vision returned. When it did, he saw a quiet, starry sky, and wispy clouds catching on the steeples and gables of Ravenby Manor. He didn't see any *Yglhfm*. He saw the smirking Princess.

"You destroyed the Dark Ones!" Yorik exclaimed.

The Princess shook her head. "Not at all," she said. "That would be a terrible thing to do!"

"Then what happened?"

"Exactly what I said would happen if they ever

came around my beautiful glade," said the Princess with immense satisfaction. She nodded toward the ground.

Yorik looked down. Now he could see, wriggling in the grass and stretching in all directions, thousands upon thousands of fat white caterpillars. "But aren't they still . . ."

"Evil?" replied the Princess. "Yes, of course, but only in a sort of limited, caterpillar way."

"What should we do with them?"

"Do with them? What do you mean, do with them?"

"We can't just leave them here," said Yorik.

"Why not?" The Princess sniffed. "They're beautiful caterpillars. Any day now they'll spin their chrysalises and turn into butterflies and fly away."

"But what about their own world? It's full of millions of Dark Ones."

"Well, it's full of caterpillars now," mused the Princess. "Sounds as though they'll rather like it there."

Yorik thought of all the floating masses of green vegetation. He hesitated, imagining a mountain-sized evil butterfly. "Still," he said, "I'd be worried about them coming back through the portal."

"I told you, they're all caterpillars," she said in irritation. "Who cares?"

"Please," said Yorik.

The Princess sighed. "Very well. For you." She reached her twig out and rapidly drew the tablet runes upon the air in silver flame. They lingered a moment, then faded, accompanied by the dead echo of a red lion's roar. She giggled. "Goodness, it's fun to do things the old-fashioned way sometimes."

"So that's it?" asked Yorik. "The portal is sealed?"

"Oh yes," said the Princess. "And forever. You can't break *my* magic with a silly hammer!"

Yorik looked up at the Manor. It seemed completely back to normal, though entirely dark, no lamps alight with all the residents gone. And the sky had no flame-blue clouds. "I don't understand why your father let them destroy his body. Why didn't he fight the Dark Ones himself?"

The Princess rolled her eyes. "Oh, it was my responsibility, really, and Father says you haven't learned how to do something properly until you've done it yourself. He's very irritating sometimes."

"My father used to say the same thing," said Yorik.

Both were quiet for a moment.

"My sister," said Yorik. "Susan was inside the wreck, in the topiary garden."

"Easy!" exclaimed the Princess. "Let's go!" She lashed out with her leafy twig. Yorik hardly had time to register the return of his right hand before the Princess seized it and they shot up into the air. The Princess's glow got brighter as they rose, with bits of silver streaming out behind her, until Yorik began to feel much like a comet.

Their comet orbited all of Ravenby Estate, high, high above.

"Erde!" shouted Yorik. "I see her!"

The age of ice on the Estate was long past, but the four hills were still there, jutting up crookedly like knees and shoulders. Two ponds made perfect eyes, and the running creek made a wide mouth that shone up at them in reflected comet glow.

"Erde, my sister!" cried the Princess. "I restore

you!" Her twig leapt, and boulders shot from the earth, and the creek seemed to bend into a smile.

"Susan!" Yorik spied the wreck of the *Indomitable,* with Lord Ravenby beside the crashed cabin, crying out the girl's name and wrenching at a smashed door with an iron rod. The door burst open, and then he was pulling her free. From thousands of feet in the air, Yorik could see the concern on Lord Ravenby's face.

"He was trying to protect her," said Yorik, proud of his sister.

"Oh, it's your little ghost friends!" said the Princess. "Do you want to say hello?"

The comet swooped down, past the wreck and over the Wooded Walk. There they saw the ghosts of Doris and Thomas standing on the path. Doris had thrown her arms around Thomas's neck and was sobbing into his shoulder.

"I'm sorry, Thomas," Doris was bawling. "I'm sorry I was such a terrible sister!"

"There, there," answered Thomas uncomfortably, patting her on the back. "You can make up for it now."

"Let's leave them alone," suggested Yorik, and the comet flew back up into the sky.

"Well," said the Princess, "what shall we do next?"

"The topiaries!" said Yorik.

The comet swooped over the garden. The fires were out, and all that remained were the charred stumps of the animals.

"Can you grow them back?" asked Yorik.

"*Can* I?" cackled the Princess. The twig shot out, and the topiary garden exploded in green.

"Rise, hare!" shouted the Princess in delirium. "Rise, all you bears and . . . animals and things!"

Before Yorik's eyes the animals grew swiftly, the topiary hare towering over them all. Then each one turned and bowed low, even the hare, toward the Princess's comet.

On a stone bench in the garden, Lord Ravenby was sitting beside Susan giving her water from a canteen. Lord Ravenby looked very tired, and Yorik worried about them finding their way home in the dark.

"Don't be concerned, Yorik," said the Princess.

She pointed the twig, and a ghostly light like a flickering lamp appeared in the forest a short distance from the humans. "There's a will-o'-the-wisp to guide them home. Your sister will know to follow it."

Susan, seeing the wisp, coaxed Lord Ravenby to his feet, and off they went along the Walk as the light receded before them, drawing them on toward Ravenby Manor.

The Princess, cometlike, glowed among the stars for several more nights before finally wheeling out of view.

After she had gone, Yorik gathered in the water garden with Doris and Thomas, and Hatch and Dye too, and the other green spirit-hounds, now beings of pure light, their physical bodies buried days ago.

The hounds seemed to know what to do without being told. They raced about, woofing and snuffling at the grass, leaping on the children and licking their hands, and tussling in the fountains. Then, as one, they made a great leap and vanished upward toward the stars.

"It's like this," explained Yorik to Doris and Thomas, looking up after the hounds. "You sort of lean back and look at the Milky Way, and see how it moves like a river. . . ."

"I do see," said Thomas, hushed.

"Me too," said Doris quietly. She took her brother's hand. "Goodbye, Yorik."

"Goodbye," said Thomas.

"Goodbye to you both, and farewell," said Yorik. He watched as brother and sister fell upward into the universe.

The water garden was quieter now. Yorik listened for a moment to the splashing of fish and frogs, and the eternal gurgle of the fountains. Then he trudged off toward the Manor.

As he went, he saw a fluttering near his arm. He looked down to see a butterfly, newly hatched from its chrysalis, its wings still wet and ragged.

"You're late," said Yorik. "All the others migrated away already. You'd better hurry after them."

He tried to shoo it away, but the butterfly didn't seem interested in moving on.

"All right." Yorik shrugged. "But you won't like

it here when winter comes." The butterfly followed him, and he left it alone.

When he reached the Manor, he climbed deftly up the wall toward a high balcony. There he shuffled along the stone balustrade until he found a generous crack. He sat atop it, waiting. The butterfly landed next to him.

The butterfly peered at him with what Yorik felt was a great deal of curiosity.

"The Princess said she would give me a great gift," explained Yorik. "The ability to choose my own ending. *Not many receive this,* she said."

The butterfly flexed its wings, almost entirely dry now.

"So I asked her if I could stay here and be a part of Erde forever. *Yes, of course,* she said. *Is that hard to do?* I asked her. *No,* said the Princess, *it's quite easy. In fact, it requires hardly any magic at all.*"

Suddenly a door opened, and from within came Susan and the Matron. Together they went to the balcony and gazed over the vast expanse of Ravenby Estate, which once again throbbed with work and life.

Then Lord Ravenby came through as well. He looked vigorous again, but also rather nervous.

"Well?" he asked Susan. "Of course, you can take the time you need to decide. But it would be my very great honor. In all that happened, you were the only one who didn't abandon me. You never left. And you need a father, and I need a daughter. . . ."

"Yes," said Susan.

"And of course I could never replace your real father, I'm sure," continued Lord Ravenby anxiously.

"Yes," said Susan, smiling and turning. "I will be your daughter. Oh! Look!" She pointed to a dandelion growing from a crack in the stone balustrade. A startled-looking butterfly was flapping nearby. "How odd," she said. "I didn't notice this before. Who would think a dandelion could grow in such a place?"

"Quite extraordinary," replied Lord Ravenby, wiping at a tear in his eye.

"Yorik told me a story about dandelions," Susan said. "He said that the seeds of a dandelion will deliver your dreams to your loved one."

And she reached out and plucked the dandelion,

and blew. And the seeds spread on the wind. They floated down to the water garden, and onto the Tropical Tell, and throughout the aviary glade, and settled even beneath the topiaries. And some of them landed in the little creek, where they drifted on the waters, along the smiling face of Erde.

acknowledgments

For all their efforts with this book, my deepest gratitude goes to Miriam Angress, J. J. Johnson, Jennifer Harrod, John Claude Bemis, Jim Thomas, Chelsea Eberly, Jason Gots, Alison Kolani, Jessica Shoffel, Ellice Lee, and Josh and Tracey Adams of Adams Literary. Also to Gris Grimly, for his inspired illustrations; Edward Gorey, whose art was a constant inspiration; and Robert Herrick, for his poem "The Night-piece, To Julia."

{about the author}

Late at night, through a hidden window, the ghost of **STEPHEN MESSER** can be seen typing away in his study, high up in the haunted manor he shares with his wife in Durham, North Carolina. In a past life, Stephen was the author of *Windblowne.* Visit Stephen online at stephenmesser.com.

{about the illustrator}

GRIS GRIMLY can best be described as a storyteller. Through his distinctive style and wide selection of media as an author, illustrator, fine artist, sculptor, and filmmaker, he has captivated a variety of loyal collectors. Primarily known for his dark yet humorous children's books, Gris continues to haunt the imaginations of both young and old. Visit him online at madcreator.com.